The FRUIT THAT CRACKED THE STONE

R E Leyland

authorHOUSE®

AuthorHouse™
1663 Liberty Drive
Bloomington, IN 47403
www.authorhouse.com
Phone: 833-262-8899

Published by AuthorHouse 09/19/2022

ISBN: 978-1-6655-7127-2 (sc)
ISBN: 978-1-6655-7126-5 (e)

Library of Congress Control Number: 2022917417

Print information available on the last page.

1

"When I call your name," spoke the authoritative professor from behind his desk. "Just respond with whatever you need to in order to indicate your presence.'

"Michael Arlen."

"Here."

"Juan Auro."

"Here."

"Cynthia Chavez."

"Here."

Methodically, the professor went down the list. The F's – the G's – the M's – the P's, not once lifting his head to make eye contact, exhibiting the fruit of his indifference and his routinized posture.

"Lisa Richardson."

"Here."

"Antonio Sanchez."

"Here."

With one more name remaining to conclude the role, the professor was compelled to pause and say the next name in his head before reciting it audibly. Having come across a wide array of names throughout his years as a professor, none had ever stood out like the one displayed before his eyes. A single word. A single name.

Finally, after a brief moment of awkward silence that disrupted the flow of systematized accountability, the name was uttered aloud.

"Tangerine."

Unlike all the other names mechanically uttered, this one was inquired and accompanied with a raised head, in an attempt to glance at the face behind the name.

"Here," softly responded a beautiful young girl who sat three rows back from the front.

The professor stared and paused for what seemed like a lengthy period of time, contributing to the already present awkwardness that had made its self known by the first distribution of silence. Emotionally, he was stirred, for the first time in years.

"And the last shall be first," he spoke to himself just above a whisper.

"No last name?" The professor went on to directly inquire, wanting to know the truth of his inquiry and wanting to rescue himself from his out of character treatment of this stranger whose role it is to just be another student.

"No last name," she spoke back with an air of confidence that exceeded her visual youthfulness mixed with tones of slight irritation as though she had had to answer that question throughout her life. "Just Tangerine."

"Interesting," stated the professor while still gazing through a stony sternness. "This is Abnormal Psychology," the professor now declared, involving the rest of the class in his audible communication while simultaneously arising from his chair. "If you're not supposed to be in this class, then I suggest you leave now. If the course you've chosen is Abnormal Psychology, then you are supposed to be here. And know this, my role sheet will be made based on where you sit today. If you do not like where you are currently sitting or who you're sitting next to, I suggest you find a place that you do like because hear me clearly, and I'll only say this once, role will be taken five minutes after the hour, no later, no sooner, and I will not call your name like I did today. I will look at your seat and if you are not in it at five minutes after the hour, then you will be considered and marked absent. No ifs, ands, or buts about it. I hope I make myself clear.'

"The format of the class and my expectations of you are thoroughly presented in the syllabus. If you have any questions regarding anything outside of the classroom lectures, save them for after class. Our time is brief and I don't want it wasted on trivial stuff."

As the professor finished, he remained in silence with his desk supporting his leaning body. The students themselves sat without a movement or a word. Seconds passed and not a budge or a sound occurred.

"Because no one moved," spoke the professor, rescuing all but himself from the menacing quietness, "I'm going to presume that you are stationed at your permanent landmark for this semester. Being apparent that is the case, if I do not find you in your current seat at five after the hour, I will consider you absent.'

"As I stated earlier, you are in Abnormal Psychology," he spoke while writing the word Abnormal Psychology on the board. "And I am Professor Patterson. And you can call me Professor Patterson."

After a lengthy lecture on the definition and history of abnormal behavior and the historical treatments of those defined as 'abnormal,' without a single question posed by the either enthralled or bored students, the professor rapped it up with a minute or two to spare. And even though the timorous pupils were foretold their permitted access of the professor's desk to inquire of him, none of them stuck around to do as such. Typical with relations to Professor Patterson's classes. With a non-approachable demeanor, most responded with scurry rather than gravitation. The preferable outcome for Professor Patterson who housed no inclinations to talk *with* students; just *at* them.

"I told you he was a prick," Lisa Richardson stated as though speaking from experience while digging in her purse to excavate a buried pack of cigarettes. "Professor Prick Patterson."

"If you think him such a prick, then why do you willingly continue to sign up for his classes?" Tangerine posed back the rational question.

"You know me," she spoke back with a sassy attitude. "I'm a glutton for punishment." (There was some truth to what Lisa spoke regarding punishment. In order to pay for her schooling, Lisa worked part time as a dominatrix – **Pain For Hire**, her services boldly advertised in the *LA Weekly* under the alias Black Magic Woman, a name she clung to after hearing the band Santana sing it through the radio airways while down in South Beach during a spring break trip). "The fact remains, prick or not, he's a brilliant professor that I learn so much from, and three courses later, my opinion of him still stands…an intellectual dick. But I have to say, in all three courses with Professor Prick, never have I seen him do what he did today. He's never look up during role. Never! When he looked at you I was surprised. I think we all were. And not just looked either, but a full on stare. Very odd."

"Odd?" Tangerine retorted back in the form of a question. "Professors make eye contact with their students. Seems pretty normal to me. You thinking it odd seems odd to me."

"With any other professor I would consider it normal. But not with Professor Prick. As I said, not once during the other courses I took did he make any eye contact during role and even when he does make eye contact during his lectures, it's like he's seeing through you and not at you. It kind'a turns me on. And come on Tangerine, you have to admit, there was an awkward silence in the room you could have cut with a knife after he called your name?"

"May I just state for the record and inform you, you're nuts!" Tangerine spoke with jovial articulation but knew within that Lisa was right. Following the announcing of her name, the classroom did become filled with an intrusive silence that couldn't be denied. "I do find him attractive though."

"Who?"

"Professor Patterson."

"Now, that's odd." Lisa blurted out just before placing the unlit cigarette into her mouth.

It wasn't odd to be attracted to Professor Patterson. It didn't necessarily breed likeability, but the facts could not be denied, he was nice on the eyes and oozed a passionate sexuality that he charismatically exhibited during his lectures on the subjects he taught. Professor Patterson had made many secret female suitors, with justifiable reasons, whose dampened panties knotted up during classroom sessions. No doubt male students had their reactions also. Professor Patterson stood around six-two, with a lean, defined, athletic build resulting from good eating habits and a regimented swimming program. Currently residing in his mid-forties, over the years, the grays had made their way through the deep, black follicles and morphed his full head of hair into a salt and pepper tone. Not necessarily displaying the process of age but more of an evolution of distinguishedness. Some would say, if it were not for a lazy left eye, physically, he would be flawless.

The lazy left eye was God's gift given to him at birth. Surgery was not an option for his parents. They couldn't afford the monetary requirements. So growing up, it had been a thorn in his side. Constant ridicules flung at him by peers and sometimes by strangers who had but a single contact with him but still verbally assaulted his physical disposition with no holds bar. To eventually fend off his foes, he acquired some street wit and boxing skills and used the one-two combo of brain and brawn to silence the mouths of those who deemed it necessary to announce in mocking fashion the obvious defect he possessed.

Over time, he accepted his fate and knew at a young age that a symmetrical face would be something he would never have. The acceptance of that reality on its terms didn't come easy. A constant presence of insecurity and self-consciousness plagued him. To compensate for his physical imperfection, Professor Patterson sought to heighten and perfect his intellect at a young age. To ascertain confidence and power through the optimizing of his mind. In his quest to do so, he had discovered that another intellectual giant had suffered from unattractiveness - (facial disfigurement) - and yet was still ever successful with the ladies, and men for that matter. However, Professor Patterson had no interest in the latter. The iconic toad of French Existentialism, Jean Paul Sartre, also had a tattered and torn eye and many other undesirable anatomical features that made him a sore sight even for good eyes. Professor Patterson clung to Sartre like a brother-in-arms and derived from him compensational inspiration. To hear Professor Patterson articulate and expose the inner workings of his mind soon made the onlooker unaware of the mild distortion scripted upon his face. A reaction he sought to design many years ago.

"I'd fuck him," Lisa stated so matter-of-factly, after taking her second drag from the cigarette. "But that's as far as I would go."

"You'd fuck anything," Tangerine wittingly stated back.

"You know me all too well."

Dear dad…

Love,
your son.

2

"I'll have a Southern Comfort and coke, on the rocks, please, and a Bud Lite in a chilled mug," Henry informed the waiter.

As the waiter departed to fetch Henry's order, the professor had approached the table and occupied the seat across from Henry.

"Good evening, Gil."

"Good evening, Henry."

"How goes the battle?" Henry inquired.

"Still rages onward."

Just then, the waiter returned with the requested drinks in hand, placing them in their designated spots, and left the two men to their own devices.

"So, how are the new academic flocks?" Henry asked prior to sipping his drink. "They all wide-eyed and bushy-tailed, waiting with baited breath to feast at your table of higher education?"

"Who knows," Gil answered apathetically, after swallowing his first swig. "Half the time I'm just lecturing and not paying attention to whom I'm even lecturing to."

"For shame, oh great one. What good is a teacher who forsakes connection with his pupils?" Henry jested with a phrase sounding more like a quote from antiquity.

"Something odd did occur today," stated Gil.

"Oh, do tell."

“It was strange. Out of the ordinary. It’s as though, I was actually emotionally moved.”

“Interesting. Very very interesting. Who was she?” Henry asked with mild enthusiasm.

“How’d you know it was a she?”

“Nothing brings a man back to life like the beauty of a woman. All the fairy tale talk of Sleeping Beauty coming back to life because of the power of a male’s kiss…it’s all patriarchal bullshit. We know it’s the woman who holds the power, not only to give us men life but also to kill us. It’s the Black Widow or Praying Mantas not the Sleeping Beauty motif that accurately depicts the personification of a woman’s power and her ability to rule over the male speci…”

“Are you finished?” Gil interrupted.

“For now. Go on.”

“Yes, it was a she, a girl. A student to be more precise. A student who goes by the name Tangerine. And get this, no last name. Just Tangerine.”

“Mmm, a nectar name. And no last name? Very very interesting. And very very seductive. Was she as tantalizing as her name is? Wow, with a name like Tangerine, one cannot help but be drawn by curiosity to witness the face behind it.”

“The name did grip my curiosity…”

“Oh, I bet it did,” Henry interrupted with what now appeared to be a turpitude grin.

“Would you mind remaining silent for just a bit, you perverted old man,” Gil rebutted back. “I’m trying to talk here. As I was saying,” the professor carried on after first swinging his elixir to help lubricate his vocal chords. “The name took me by surprise, actually causing me, out of curiosity, to, as you said, view the face behind the name. Well, once I looked upon this so-called Tangerine, I was fixed on her like a deer in headlights. First of all, I rarely, if ever, look up from my role sheet to peer at the students I call and never, in all my years of teaching, have I stared at a student, in this case, stared into a student for what felt like an obvious, lengthy period of time, one in which all the other students got to witness and I suspect, feel. I have no idea how long I was captured by her. It could have been a second or an eternity. Time seemed suspended."

"Good for you," Henry stated, affirming goodness on what Gil implicitly deemed an act of foolery. "It's about time you stared into someone rather than steering away from someone."

"That's good, Mr. Professor," Gil jeered back. "You have a way with words."

"Why thank you, my eager apprentice," Henry ping-ponged back. "I take it she was quite striking?"

"All that you could image a girl named Tangerine would look like and more. Even an imagination like yours."

"Sounds to me like the sweet nectar of this Tangerine has bitten you with a temptress kiss."

"I would hardly qualify an emotional reaction as an allurement towards another."

"Say what you will, but keep in mind, before Adam ate the fruit, he was first reactively stirred by the woman."

"Oh, now you're comparing me to Adam and the simple act of raising my head during role calling equivalent to the Paradise Lost drama of Eden."

And though Gil tried to verbally minimize the encounter with the single-name student, deep within, the stirrings he initially experienced were now stirring again as a result of discussing the experience itself.

"You're right," Henry interjected. "I'm being melodramatic. I'm just glad to hear that emotions still exist within you. That you're not some pre-programmed robot. Some post-stoic philosopher that resides solely in your head. And who knows, maybe this reactive stirring just might lead to some kind of emotional resurgence and be the very catalyst to get you to respond to a certain someone."

"Please, it'll take a whole lot more than a reactive stirring to crack this stone and compel me to do what I know I should do."

"It's a start," Henry uttered with hope in his voice.

"I received another one yesterday," the professor stated in a sullen voice knowing full well Henry knew what he was referring to.

"And?"

"And nothing. I read it, was stricken with guilt and shame, and then stuck it the drawer with all the other ones."

"Anything new?"

"He's about to graduate from fifth grade. The school is having some kind of a ceremony which he would like me to attend," Gil said while staring into his glass of beer with his index finger tapping the rim.

"Will you attend?" Henry reluctantly posed the question after a momentary pause knowing full well his question was a rhetorical one.

"We both know I won't. I'm not ready to even write a letter. Where would I find the strength to look upon him?"

"The same way you looked upon this Tangerine girl."

"Please Henry, now you're comparing apples to oranges."

"Apples to Tangerines."

Henry's statement brought a mutual chuckle out of both of them, dissipating the melancholy that was creeping its way into their dyad dialogue. Gil raised his head from his fixed gaze on the beer with a partial smile streaking his face, greeted with a reciprocal expression from Henry. The two touched glasses as a nonverbal expression of care and love for one another that has extended throughout the decade.

They would meet again, next Tuesday evening: same place, same time, same drinks, just as it's been for the past many, many years.

3

Black, tight leather housed the taut, youthful, curvaceous anatomy of the Black Magic Woman. The grip of the whip resided perfectly in her tiny feminine but strong right hand. The left hand lassoed by the cowhide leash sporadically yanked with dominating authority. Attached to the opposite end, submissively on all fours like an unevolved animal, was Dr. Honowski, the head ER physician affiliated with the Presbyterian Hospital in Whittier, California. Dr. Honowski has been one of the Black Magic Woman's regulars for the past two years. Two times a month, sometimes more, depending on his need for a stress release.

"Moan, you little bitch," the dark specimen-of-pain commanded the helpless creature while cracking her whip on the thin cotton covered derriere of Dr. Honowski.

Something undecipherable was reactively uttered shortly after the leathery material snapped and no doubt, marked the fair, tender skin of a concealed ass cheek with a red, soon-to-be welt. Dr. Honowski's native English dialect could not be clearly articulated through the plastic ball barricading his mouth and securely positioned by straps tightly fastened around his head. By the third lash, the doctor exhaled a yelp of increased volume, communicating a fine mixture of pleasure and pain.

The hour session was over. Dr. Honowski had received his money's worth. Multiple red welts scathed his buttocks, pinkish hued indentations paved his facial cheeks as marked remnants of a tight yanked leash and underwear filled with semen. All a recipe for purchased satisfaction.

Dr. Honowski left room 6 of the Travel Lodge while the Black Magic Woman remained behind. Derobing her super-villain costume and civilizing herself, Lisa soon checked out of her hour and half borrowed hotel room and drove home with a good feeling of economical satisfaction.

The pleasing of customers through dominating means never gave Lisa personal sexual satisfaction, but it did, however, arouse her to the point of wanting to get off. Being one deeply involved in the secret underground world of forbidden sexual fetishes, Lisa became conditioned to experience orgasms either through the high road of lovemaking, which had been an ancient act for her conducted years ago, or by the debased path of necrophilia. For the time being, Lisa was not in love. So tonight, she would get off by facially fucking the dead.

"Todd," Lisa spoke through her cell phone while in route to the morgue. "Hey, it's me. Lisa."

"Hey, Lisa," responded an apathetic voice from the other end.

"I'm on my way to see you. Any availability?"

"Yeah. We just got a fresh one in. A middle-aged fella with a mustache."

"I'll be there in about thirty minutes."

"Well hurry, I'm leaving in about two hours."

"Come through the back, right?"

"Knock. Or call me when you're in the parking lot."

"Thanks, Todd, see ya soon."

"Yeah. Okay. Bye."

"Bye."

Lisa blazed her way towards her destination. The green light had been given and her sexual, kinky desires were free to run rampant. The mustache was an unexpected but added bonus to be used to rub against and stimulate the clitoris while the nose of the dead vanished inside her already wet vagina.

Lisa had met Todd Palermo at her local Blockbuster where he used to work part time before becoming a full time diener at a mortuary. After discovering Lisa had a pattern of renting dark, scary slasher movies, Todd had broached the subject of her interest in the macabre and soon a relationship developed between them that was essentially connected by their mutual fascination with death. Over time, the willful unveiling of their inner selves occurred. Todd confessed his gay tendencies and his reoccurring visits to local bathhouses where he indulged himself in coitus acts with multiple strangers. He also confided his fetish for mannequins and his midnight masturbation rendezvous with his lifeless friend he called Harold who he concealed behind the hanging clothes in his bedroom closet. Lisa, in return, shared her erotic tendency towards the deceased and longed for the opportunity to sexually fiddle with the dead. With Todd being entrusted with keys to the mortuary and hours of toil all alone, he had provided Lisa the chance to gratify her wish and fully discover her inner alter ego's appetite for necrophilia. One time was all it took and she was hooked. Since that initial encounter, Todd and Lisa had consented that whenever she had an urge to face-fuck a corpse and Todd had availability and a cadaver, he would provide her access to the dead for some alone time to gratify her lecherous libido.

Todd's cell phone rang. Lisa's name appeared on the screen.

"I'm in the parking lot," Lisa informed Todd.

"I'll unlock the back door. Just walk in."

In a matter of minutes, Lisa was in. Todd sealed and locked the door behind her and pointed to the room where the deceased Hector Espinoza laid lifeless on a table awaiting his placement into the nice, oak casket his family struggled to purchase days ago. Mr. Espinoza was a handsome, forty-seven-year old man who "unexpectedly died" of a heart attack just under a week ago. (It is quite certain that the excessive alcohol and nicotine intake contributed to his heart calling it quits). Tonight, he will have the youngest vagina residing on his face he'd ever had throughout his whole life. Unfortunately, for Mr. Espinoza, his lifeless tongue and other inoperative senses will not experience the delicacies of Lisa's spilling sexuality. Only she will be the recipient of delight granted by the cold immobility of Mr. Espinoza. And little will anyone know, after Todd completes the clean up of Lisa's tryst, that the departed they look upon during the open casket ceremony had been recently assaulted by the genitalia of a strange, young woman.

Todd gave Lisa forty-five minutes max. He had things to do and wasn't going to delay them for her. Forty-five minutes was more than enough time. Lisa was so sexually charged by her punishment of Dr. Honowski and the anticipation of a cold nose penetrating her wet, warm vagina that just the sight of the mustache-face corpse was practically enough to get her off.

Though cut short by Todd's prior engagement, Lisa's sexual ritual with the dead would not be altered. A ritual she had designed and developed over time.

Round and round, she circled the lifeless entity like a stocking beast taunting a helpless, wounded prey, prolonging the inevitable pouncing. Two to three times she went around Mr. Espinoza while removing her garments, each circular rotation heightening the primal incantation and the bestial urge to attack and devour. By the third revolution, she was completely naked. With cat-like agility, she leaped and straddled the pale, cold creature's bare chest and let the icy, tingling skin heat up her inner thighs and further moisten that which lies in between. Collapsing her upper torso and landing her chest onto the expressionless face, she frantically rubbed with frenzied friction each breast all over and around Mr. Espinoza's non-reactive mug, ending the jubilant assault with slow, sensual traces of his facial structure with each erected nipple.

Nearly peaking the threshold of primitive delight, she flung herself up to the head and sat, targeting the nose with sniper-like precision to have it disappear into her dripping vagina. Upon insertion, climax occurred. With further gyrations, another. To conclude and experience a few more orgasms with greater intensity, Lisa turned around to utilize Mr. Espinoza's mustache as an instrument for clitoris stimulation while simultaneously being fucked by his nose. The two anatomical features worked in harmonious unison to bring about the crescendo Lisa predetermined. The effusion of it all left her powerless to resist the crumbling of herself into the lower portion of Mr. Espinoza's body, delectably collapsing in to a 69-position.

"Todd," Lisa hollered into the dimly lit hallway after she had regained her composure and dressed herself. Now, stepping into the dimly lit hallway, she implored once more, "Todd."

"Down here" harkened back, a distant voice without a physical being to be seen.

"I'm all done," Lisa stated as though speaking about a typical task like eating all the veggies on a dinner plate before allowed to eat the dessert.

"Just let yourself out the back. I'll clean up when I get the chance."

"Thanks, Todd," Lisa yelled as she approached the door she originally entered so as to exit from. "We'll talk soon."

No other voice was heard.

Lisa saw her way out, got into her car, and headed home in a state of fain contentment. Upon checking her phone, displayed were one missed call and four voicemails. Two of the calls were from first timers seeking sexual services from the *LA Weekly* ad, another from a regular wanting some late night gratification, and the last from Tangerine in need of some academic assistance regarding Abnormal Psychology. Lisa bypassed the two newcomers, postponed calling the regular, and immediately contacted Tangerine. Only after discussing at length the next day's assignment with Tangerine did Lisa arrange and meet up with another of her regulars for a late night rendezvous.

Dear dad…

Love,
your son

4

Thursday morning and already three weeks into the semester. Tuesdays and Thursdays Professor Patterson taught Abnormal Psychology. Today's topic of lecture would be on the DSM-IV, diagnosing, and mood disorders.

Passion for teaching was the one true emotion that Professor Patterson permitted to stay after the tragedy. Had it not been for the innate component of human self-preservation and his *causa-sui* project to mold the minds of others, the deep end would have sucked him in and annihilated his life completely. Beyond the safeguarding of self and the educational mission of others, all else had been relinquished and detached from the care and love of Professor Patterson, even the fruit of the womb - the descendant seed that survived during delivery.

However, since that moment during role call when eye contact was made with the so-called Tangerine, unexpected emotions were making their unwanted climb to the surface. Excitement, sometimes accompanied with fantasy, made its way to the forethought of the Professor's brain and permeated visceral charges throughout his body. Seeing Tangerine every Tuesday and Thursday during class only exasperated his newly found abnormal condition, resulting in an obvious all-to-often peering her way during classroom lectures. This behavior – overt peering - was out of sorts and out of character for him that seemed to serve as added fuel to an already unwanted lit fire and helped leverage for Lisa Richardson her argument that Professor Patterson's out of the norm behavior was because of Tangerine. Initially, Tangerine thought Lisa was being a bit dramatic, but soon came to grips with the obvious and found the whole thing flattering and Professor Patterson even more appealing.

As he drove in route to the campus, in his head Professor Patterson went over his attire and pondered if the faded jeans, the mildly tattered Nimrod sandals he got on his first of three trips to Israel and the newly purchased short sleeve, button up, beige shirt would be an outfit magnetic enough to catch an eye. More specifically, Tangerine's eye.

Without the attribute of care came the freedom from second guessing. Such freedom was becoming lost on the Professor the more Tangerine was thought of. An outfit for admiration was, at one time, the least of Professor Patterson's concerns. Now, he's purchasing new shirts and assembling daily outfit-ensembles, something he did several years ago but gave up the giving-of-shit when the most valuable thing was taken from him.

Nothing good could become of what he was thinking, feeling and starting to do. Teachers don't get involved with their students. It's forbidden. And yet, it was already occurring. Attaching is the beginning of involvement. Conscious decisions on what to wear and anticipated excitement on particular days due to a particular individual are symptoms of attachment formation. This starting point leading to nowhere was nothing but an adolescent crush, so thought the Professor, and yet, an insignificance he couldn't seem to help. He knew it to be wrong and silly but continued to play into it. It was getting to the point that even on Mondays, Wednesdays, and Fridays, he second guessed his adorned garments just in case an unexpected encounter happened during a campus crossing of Tangerine's path.

Another bizarre development that was beginning to take place within Professor Patterson that confirmed his unwanted developmental attachment towards Tangerine was his desire for her to stick around after class and approach his desk for some post-lecture inquiries. Mind-you, this was out of character for him due to the fact that he had developed dread for any after class interactions with students over the latter dark years.

Thus far, into the semester, Tangerine had made no steps towards his desk.

"After the break," Professor Patterson spoke after concluding his thought provoking discussion on symptoms and proper diagnosing of mental disorders, "we'll go over mood disorders."

The students rose and scurried, some stretching their legs while others headed off to attack the vending machines. Lisa and Tangerine were part of the assaulting squad, aiming to tie over their bellies with high-priced vending delicacies. Professor Patterson had no qualms with eating in his class as long as the sounds of calorie intake didn't muffle out or disrupt the sound of his voice during lectures.

"Did ya notice his new shirt?" Lisa inquired of Tangerine about Professor Patterson's upper attire, demonstrating her sixth sense for fashion and her ongoing acknowledgement of Professor Patterson's new and improved behavior.

"I did notice how sexy he looks today, but I couldn't tell you if the shirt was new or not. And how would you know? Been stalking his closet?"

"Trust me, I know men and I have had enough courses with Professor Patterson to see into his closet and clearly detect that within the last few weeks, he has upgraded his fashion sense with what seems to be an attempt to impress. He could do without those funky sandals though."

"I like them," Tangerine interjected in a subtle tone of defense. "I think they're called Nimrods, footwear only made in Israel. I actually have a pair that I've outgrown but still hold onto them for keepsake."

"Now, how would you know the brand of sandals he wears?"

"Trust me, I know shoes."

They both laughed and proceeded to purchase their food items and head back for the second half of the class and Professor Patterson's – no doubt – stimulating lecture.

"Karl Marx, the ingenious humanitarian and not the Red-Threat to democracy as the perversion of Russian communism depicted and the West did and still does interpret Marxism to be, once said," Professor Patterson charismatically spoke while writing down the following Marx quote on the whiteboard. "'I am nothing and should be everything.' By the way, to get a better understanding of the man Karl Marx and his Communistic doctrine, I recommend you read Erich Fromm's *Chains of Illusion*." This was typical tangent behavior from Professor Patterson. He had a habit of provided his students with a plethora of suggested readings when he came across sections in his lectures that sparked insightful resources that would further educate his pupils outside the classroom. Professor Patterson's motto as an educator from the get-go has been to plant seeds and not just bear fruit.

"Yes, Lisa?" the Professor inquired, responding to Lisa's raised arm.

"What was the author's name again, please?" Although Lisa had what some may label as lecherous desires and judge as debased mischievous conduct, even immoral, she was a diligent student and had a strong love for learning.

"Erich Fromm," he replied, this time writing the name on the whiteboard and the title of the mentioned book. "What Karl Marx was saying, whether he knew it or not, that this 'what I am' and 'what I should be' is the essential formula for depression, especially if you're viewing your client, or even yourself for that matter, from a cognitive modality. Most, if not, all individuals question and struggle with who they are, especially in light of who they think they should be. This condition is only exasperated in a capitalistic system that depends on progress in order to survive.'

"Capitalism is sustained and one would say thrives when individuals within that system are consuming. Aldous Huxley once said, 'When the individual feels, the community reels.' Erich Fromm, the individual I mentioned earlier, stated in a portion of his book titled *The Art Of Loving*, - (*again, writing the title of the book on the whiteboard*) - when speaking about love and its disintegration within a capitalistic system, 'The world is one big object for our appetite: a big apple, a big bottle, a big breast; we are the sucklers, the eternal expected ones, the eternal hopeful ones, and the eternal disappointed ones.' In order for there to be consumption, the human creature must be conditioned to want and need. And it's even better when the human creature believes his wants are his needs. This is where advertisement comes into play and manipulates through propagated sensationalism, falsifying information so as to condition the human creature to believe that they need things they can't afford to impress people they don't even know or possibly even like and to attempt to be someone they really aren't. And what you have and who you were yesterday seems irrelevant for today. Yesterday is old news. What you have and what you are today is all that matters. Progress. Everything is progress. Continued evolution. Restless striving. Hence why anxiety is a normalized epidemic. And, we as a society, buy into this type of collective thinking, even though deep within we, as a people, suffer from neurotic behavior and live in depressive states, anxious states, unhealthy states, predominantly due to the fact that we have been conditioned to strive for and always fall short of the 'what we should be' while anxiously and neurotically fighting to be saved from the disparity of the inner self-deprecating accuser that says 'I am nothing' – (*now, writing this phrase on the whiteboard*). And the further the chasm between the two polar concepts of 'I am nothing'- (*under lining the written phrase on the whiteboard*) - and 'should be everything' – (*now, writing this phrase on the whiteboard and under lining it*), often times the greater the depression. In Freudian terminology, this would be a split or in Jungian lingo it would be considered an inner cleavage, the seedbed for pathological neuroses. This means that if the etiology of depression is based on what I just formulated, then prognosis lies in the synthesizing of the two polar opposites, and the closer the two come together, holism over dualism, a healthier wholeness will inevitably result, placing and leaving the human creature in its originally designed state. The state of being, or as Martin Heidegger called Dasein (*now, writing that word on the whiteboard*) rather than a constant and chronic becoming.'

"Any questions?" Professor Patterson asked the students, his typical *modus operandi* fifteen minutes prior to class ending.

Sure enough, many hands were raised as was the typical student MO that followed the Professor's thought evoking lectures. However, when the fifteen minutes was up, wherever the discussion was, it was cut off for promptness of dismissal. Class started on time and finished on time; rarely, if ever, any exceptions.

Class concluded and Professor Patterson took his usual seat behind his desk while the students gathered their academic gear and prepared for departure. Professor Patterson preoccupied his behavior by appearing to re-organize the pell-mell that became his desk by the end of each class. Little did others know, that inside, Professor Patterson waited with hopeful anticipation that Tangerine would stick around to, at this point, inquire about anything. While laboring away - restoring order from scattered chaos - he quickly glanced up to inconspicuously catch glimpses of the status of Tangerine's doings. The last glance caught her backside heading for the door. In moments, she, like all the others, was gone.

Disappointment again. The very reason why Professor Patterson loathed the unwanted attachment that had formed to Tangerine. Emotional freedom was regressing to the captive shackles of desire. Not to the cradling place of pleasure. Rather, to the vexed chamber of pain.

The only hope of absolving the pangs resulting from his uncontrollable expectations was through talk therapy. Henry would have to be called upon for an emergency Thursday night dialogue and drinks. Out of the norm but a decree of on-call friendship that had been established between them years ago and periodically used. Henry would have to cancel his prescheduled nine o'clock appointment without even a second thought. Henry's friend was primary. Animalistic carnality would have to be delayed.

Meanwhile, the day carried on. Beneath the autumn sky and a cluster of Sycamore trees, Professor Patterson relaxed in the shade they were naturally providing. It was his location for lunch. A prime piece of campus real estate he - and once his other - would occupy, providing a cross breeze and a panoramic view of the school grounds. Alone, he would eat his brought-from-home-self-made meal. Just the way he liked it. No disturbances and no money spent. Many times during his great escape into his reclusive solace, female admirers would approach him in attempts to befriend the professor they had a crush on. He was cordial but preferred to eat and be left alone.

From where they sat – (Tangerine, Lisa, and their third party friend, Rimy Decado) - Professor Patterson could be easily spotted. It wasn't the norm for the fem-trio to park their derrieres on this portion of the campus. The weather of the day made it just right for an outdoor gathering. Lisa sparked the idea and the others thought it grand.

Lounging and basking beneath an October sky, the three ladies ate and conversed. Nothing of grave, serious nature. Predominately twaddle talk.

"Hey, isn't that Professor Patterson over there?" Tangerine inquired of the other two.

"Where?" Lisa inquired in return, having her back to where he was.

"There," Tangerine responded now pointing. "Beneath those trees."

"Yeah," Rimy peeped in, possessing the same view as Tangerine. "He's there a lot."

"Aww…he's all by himself," Lisa said aloud with a tone that balanced between sympathy and sarcasm.

"Whenever I've seen him out here, most of the time he's been alone," spoke Rimy. "On a few occasions, I've seen some students talking with him. All of them females, of course."

"I'm surprised," Tangerine said. "He comes across as the type that doesn't want to be bothered outside of class. Even in class, he seems like he doesn't want to be bothered. So many times I've wanted to approach him after class to ask questions, but he seems so unapproachable."

"Tangerine wants to fuck him," Lisa stated.

"Really?" Rimy responded.

"No. Don't pay any attention to her."

"I would," Lisa proudly proclaimed.

"And that's a shock?" Rimy said back as one who knew Lisa all too well but not to the paraphilias depths as Tangerine knew her.

"Well, I'm sure he wants to fuck you," Lisa said, speaking about Tangerine.

"Once again, you've gone mad," Tangerine retaliated.

"Rimy, you should see the way Professor Patterson stares at her during class. This is my third course with him and he has never, in any of the classes I've taken, eyed someone as much as he has been eyeing Tangerine. And God knows I've tried to provoke him to notice me with skimpy skirts and my tits nearly falling out of my tops. But the way he looks at Tangerine, you'd think she was naked."

"I'll admit," Tangerine speaking up, "since you've pointed it out to me, I've noticed it. But it's not like he's gawking at me like the way you're making it out to be."

"Say what you want Tangerine, he wants you. What guy wouldn't, you're hot. I'm a straight girl and I'm turned on by you."

"Shut up!" Tangerine declared.

"Can we just agree that he may, just possibly, have some kind of attraction or crush on you?"

"Agreed. But all the other shit is a stretch of your dirty imagination."

"You should consider it a compliment the things I'm saying. I would love to be *that* teacher's pet," Lisa said.

"What about his eye though," Rimy pointing out the obvious. "Doesn't it creep you out a bit?"

Lisa knew that compared to the things that turned her on, Professor Patterson was a flawless Adonis. "I guess, after a while, you forget it's even there."

"I don't know how one would ever forget that defect. It would always be in your face."

"Obviously, I noticed it the first day of class," Tangerine chimed in. "But like Lisa said, after a while, it seems to fade away, especially when you become so enamored by his intellect."

Tangerine had known all too well about facial marring. All her life, she had stared at, caressed, and kissed the partially deformed face of her father, who, not once did she ever consider unattractive. In fact, Tangerine's father was the most beautiful man she knew, regardless of his facial imperfection. He, still a youngster without wife or child, was in attendance at the Altamont Speedway free concert put on by the Rolling Stones back in 1969. Near the stage, he was caught up in the mayhem that occurred when the Hell's Angels, who bounced for the Stones, began to enforce their power onto the crowd with an iron fist. Standing near Meredith Hunter, the eighteen-year-old black male who was killed, Tangerine's father was in harms way and a recipient of the brutal over-spill, freakishly being struck by something, still unknown till this day, that sliced open and paralyzing the right side of his face, eventually leaving it in a state of drooping disposition. The unfortunate price he paid for front rows seats. Tangerine's mother,

Sienna Monet at the time before changing it to Sienna Monet Acosta, fell in love with Tangerine's father instantly and not once wrestled with the disfigurement of his face. Tangerine, like her mother, became the fruit that didn't fall far from the tree and beheld beauty where it truly laid; from within.

"Even beyond the face," Rimy spoke, "he's kinda odd."

"More mysterious than odd," Lisa reframing Rimy's perspective. "Making him even more sexy."

"I kind'a agree with Rimy," Tangerine said. "A man so full of passion and charisma when lecturing and then lifeless in comparison once the lectures finish. He comes across as one who doesn't practice what he preaches. He seems deeply disturbed. Not the creepy, psycho-killer disturbed. More of the deep, wounded disturbed."

"I'm sure you know about his wife and child?" Rimy posed what she deemed a rhetorical question.

"No," Tangerine said.

"I know bits of the story," Lisa interjected.

"You knew he had a wife and child and you didn't tell me," Tangerine spoke at Lisa.

"Since when are you interested in the personal lives of professors? See Rimy, she wants to fuck him."

"It's not that at all. I've never seen him wear a wedding band."

"He was married," Rimy stated, correcting Tangerine's assumptions. "The story is…he had been married, supposedly to a beautiful woman who also used to teach here. It's said they were the faculty sweethearts that students used to surround and have a lot of after class interactions with. In fact, again, the story goes, Professor Patterson and his then bride spent their lunch hours beneath that same tree were he's sitting now and supposedly flocks of students used to join them for lunch and freely interact about everything. Beneath that tree was the campus hot spot for free higher education provided by the Pattersons. So the man you now experience…the dead man as you put it, Tangerine, supposedly would be the same passionate and charismatic man even outside of the classroom setting…fun, loving, out-going and approachable; the very opposite of all that he seems to be now."

"What happened to his marriage?" Tangerine asked.

"It's said," Rimy furthering the narrative, "she died giving birth to their only child."

"Oh my God!" Tangerine responding with a deep tone of sympathy. "How horrible!"

"Supposedly the son survived but no one has ever seen him," Rimy carried on. "The rumors are, the boy was given up for adoption or granted legal guardianship to an aunt from the wife's side."

"Supposedly," Lisa throwing in her portion of the puzzle. "The school gave Professor Patterson a year off with pay to grieve over his loss. But even then, rumor has it, it took him a while to get back in the swing of things."

"It's said that he's never been the same since," Rimy said.

"Well, who would be," Tangerine uttered. "My God…the poor man. It all makes sense. How he is. The contrast between the two ways he acts. Because when he lectures, I feel his humanity, a type of connection. He's very dynamic…very alluring. Captivating. After, he's gone, like the person who taught vanished and the other person shows up, cold, distant, unapproachable and it's not because he's a prick, as you introduced him to me as," speaking to Lisa. "It's because he's numb, detached in order to survive. What a tragic story. Now I feel sorry for Professor Patterson.'

"When did this happen?" Tangerine inquiring of the other two.

"Supposedly years ago…like around five or so." Rimy said.

"What I don't understand," Lisa spoke up, "if all the rumors, or whatever you want to call them, are true and that very tree he's lying under was the meeting ground for he and his wife, why would he spend time there? It would be emotional suicide for me. I think I'd want to avoid that spot at all cost."

"It makes perfect sense," Tangerine interjected. "It's a place of fondness that probably holds great memories, which in return keeps her alive and near to him. I imagine him conversing with her while he's there. Her ghost could be his companion. Maybe that's why he's alone. Maybe he wants to be alone in order to be alone with her. And yet, it still saddens me to see him there by himself…alone"

Tangerine now saw the Professor in a whole different light. She understood his behavior and didn't hold it against him like Lisa or Rimy seemed to do, and probably many others. The sympathy she was struck to the core with oddly morphed into a deeper attraction, beyond the one she had already acquired sparked by his intellect and natural appealing looks.

It's as though she wanted to save him.

"Maybe you should go over there and see if he would like some company," Lisa wittingly said to Tangerine.

"Maybe," Tangerine responded through a hazed stare directed towards where Professor Patterson laid. "Just not today."

The Thursday night crowd was not much different than the Tuesday night crowd. Mostly locals. A few vagabonds playing pool and drinking pitchers of beer. A stone's throw away from the clashing sounds of pool balls and celebratory antics of intoxicated pool players, Henry and Gil occupied their Tuesday night location, with their usual drinks in hand.

"My mind is very much preoccupied with her," Gil said with tones of frustration. "Only perpetuating the attachment I'm so fervently trying to resist."

"What's there to resist?" Henry asked before polishing off the last of his Southern Comfort and Coke. "You're male, she's female…it's all natural mathematics, two plus two equals four."

"Spoken like a true cultural anthropologist," Gil said. "I wish it were as simple as two plus two. However, I don't feel, remember? And I don't want to feel, especially for a student. I'm involuntarily attracted to the impossible knowing full well it will and can go nowhere."

"And how do you know, oh great foreteller of the future?"

"First of all, I don't want this. Second, teachers have rules, one being, not to get relationally involved with the students outside of the teacher-student dynamic."

"Bah-hum-bug. Since when are you a rule man? We both know you are a rebel by nature. An advocate for freedom. It's what stands you out apart from the crowd and is the cornerstone of our friendship. And don't tell me all the female students that have practically begged you to have sex with them were rejected by you because of some stupid policy. I know you Gil, you're not the ethicist type. The only reason you never gave into their advancements was your emotional detachment to everything and within that posture you instilled a fortitude, not to resist, but rather not to care, possibly making others think you to be some strong moralist who had the will to evade temptation. The problem you're having now is that emotions are rearing their ugly head and the laws of attraction…well my definition of laws of attraction are strongly coming into play and your only solution, or shall I say, cheap ass excuse is to fall back on some hogwash school policy you don't even believe in. You're so full of shit and don't want to admit it. You've always said, the worst deception is self deception."

"And what am I suppose to do, oh great informer of truth? Walk up to her after class and say, 'Excuse me, I know I'm more than likely old enough to be your father, besides the fact that I am also your professor, but I was wondering if you'd like to have dinner sometime?' Yeah, I'm sure that would go over well. I don't need that additional scenario playing in my head. It's bad enough hoping that at the end of each class she sticks around to ask me questions. You know, I catch myself looking up from my desk to see what route she's taking when the class ends, hoping each time she's heading towards my desk. And so far, every time she's left the room and I'm left feeling like even more of a fool…a dumb ass."

"Fool or not, I'm just glad you're feeling. I'm telling you Gil, when resistance tampers with the laws of attraction, madness results. I think it was Oscar Wilde who said that the best way to deal with temptation is to give into it."

"Boy, Henry, that all sounds like a recipe for success. You should be a life coach."

"Say what you will, but remember, madness only increases when the laws of attraction's natural flow is disrupted; when a man's desires exceed accessibility to gratify them…and in your case Gil, I have to say, a bleeding heart is preferred over a beating heart."

"Another good one Shakespeare. No…let me guess…Oscar Wilde?"

"No…me."

5

With her nine o'clock cancellation, a window of opportunity was granted to a new customer. Another John Doe wanting some painful pleasure served up from a hot dish. The nine thirty in-call appointment had been prearranged around eight o'clock and Lisa was in route with S&M gear riding shotgun. Along with the Black-Magic-Woman leather suit, whips, handcuffs, chains, and leash all concealed in a Nike bag was her trusty bodyguard; a handheld can of mace for those unexpected brutes that don't understand the meaning of "no" or "stop" who may pose a threat to Lisa's well being. The risk of consensual abuse, especially with first timers.

Two hundred and fifty dollars richer and an hour an a half after being welcomed into the elaborate home of the new John Doe, who's wife's weekend retreat with the church gave him an opportunity to live out his dark repressed fetish, Lisa returned to her civilian attire and was heading home from a job well done. Customer satisfaction was her business mission statement and between the yelping, crying, and cuming, Lisa knew her fragile first timer got his money's worth.

Displayed on her cell phone was a new voice message. It was from Tangerine.

When you get this, call me. Don't worry about the time. I have a question that's been going through my head all evening and I'm hoping you have an answer for it. Bye.

"Hello," Tangerine picked up on the other end sounding wide awake regardless of it now being eleven twenty at night.

"Did I wake you?" Lisa inquired.

"No, I'm just taking a break from reading chapter twenty-three. You know me, trying to stay ahead."

"Well ahead I'd say. That's for next Tuesday's class right?"

"Yeah. Some interesting stuff. Sexual disorders. I'm sure we could find some symptoms in that chapter to diagnose you. …Where are you?"

"Heading back from a job."

"The professor?" Tangerine asked, knowing the inside scoop of Lisa's liaisons, but not the knowledge of what professor. Lisa's tittering-balance between disclosure and maintaining anonymity.

"No. He canceled. A first timer."

"How'd it go?"

"Fine. No problems. Business as usual."

A little over a year ago, Lisa had confided in Tangerine about how she was making her money. Not without initial hesitancy. Lisa feared judgment and rejection from Tangerine and to her pleasant surprise received just the opposite. Tangerine was understanding and very non-judgmental. Eventually, Tangerine became inquisitive, which in return, Lisa indulged her with details. Lisa, at one point, presented Tangerine with an employment opportunity in the same field, maybe shadowing her for a few trysts, a sort of dynamic duo, and then eventually branching out on her own. Tangerine passed on the proposal but remained highly interested in Lisa's occupational encounters and even more interested in Lisa's safety.

"I'm glad to hear you're safe. Are you done for the night?"

"Yeah," Lisa responded with warmth in her heart for Tangerine's concerns. "You said you had a question for me."

"Yeah. You know today when me, you, and Rimy were talking about Professor Patterson…"

"Just can't seem to get him off your mind, huh?" Lisa interrupted.

"I guess not. What I've been wondering, something we didn't talk about in more detail was his kid. You have any idea why the kid is not with him? You guys did say the kid was given away for adoption. I don't get it. Why? Was it really not his kid? Did they do some kind of DNA testing and discover the child belonged to another man? Or was Professor Patterson abusive or neglectful and social services had to remove the kid? These are the theories I've been pondering and as you can tell, have only resulted in more questions. So if you could shed any light on this, maybe I could stop obsessing."

"I would love to help you, sweetie, but rumors about the child didn't seem to fly as much as the info about his deceased wife. Speculations arose, but beyond that, nothing. I guess you're left with two options: either continue obsessing or ask him yourself."

"Yeah right. 'Excuse me professor, we've never talked one on one, but I just wanted to know why the child you had with your now dead wife is no longer being raised by you?' Great idea Lisa! Next Tuesday after class, I think I'll follow your suggestion."

"Well then, I guess you're left to obsess."

"You're always so helpful."

"It's what I do, aim to help and please others."

"And you do it so well."

"Why, thank you."

"You're welcome. Goodnight, witchie-woman."

"Good night, bitchie-girl." Lisa clicked and concluded their dialogue.

Dear dad…

Love,

your son.

6

"Paraphilias means love beyond the usual," Professor Patterson spoke aloud to the students while writing the word *philia* for love and *para* for beyond the usual on the whiteboard. "This could encompass many facets of sexual behavior. Fetishes, homosexuality, transsexuality, transgender, pedophilia, necrophilia, bestiality, and the list goes on."

"Professor Patterson," Tangerine spoke up without a raised hand. "How can you lump homosexuality together with pedophilia and consider them the same? Can't homosexuality be simply two individuals of the same sex in love, consensual adults in an egalitarian relationship, whereas pedophilia is essentially a slave-master dynamic?"

"Great observation, Tangerine. How about the rest of you, agree or disagree with Tangerine's observation?"

"Could it be," a young man in the back responded, "although homosexuality may not be as wrong as pedophilia, but still be considered a love beyond the usual?"

"For that matter," Professor Patterson broke in, "masturbation could be considered a paraphilia. It's what I've been saying all along, abnormality is subjective. This means, there can be social sanctions against certain behaviors, indirectly forming within the conscious or subconscious mind a standard for social normality. Some would think that if those sanctions are transgressed then abnormal behavior has occurred and pathology has come into play. However, private sanctions may transgress social sanctions and still be okay for the so-called transgressor. Kierkegaard once said, 'Even if what I believe in is objectively false, it can be subjectively true.' Same goes for human sexuality. What others deem as abnormal – love beyond the usual – I may be fine with it. Some religious sects preach masturbation to be considered sin, while others engage in the act of self-gratification several times a week and live with a clear conscience. Believe it or not, there are individuals who may have sex with the dead, which there are social sanctions against, who have no emotional or psychological impairment as a result."

Lisa's ass cheeks reactively clinched in to a defensive posture upon hearing Professor Patterson make his educational point with the willful delights one can experience with necrophilia. She would have loved to confirm Professor Patterson's statement but thought it best not to be transparent about her desire for the dead and her historical liaisons with cold corpses. Instead, she privately and silently "amen-ed" Professor P. and opted not to let the rest of the classroom congregates know that he was preaching to the choir.

"There was a time during the Roman Empire when the Caesars had, basically, boy toys that the society didn't frown upon. In fact, considered it quite normal. Homosexuality was ramped within the Roman aristocracy. Orgies. Incest. The whole gamut. Sexual behaviors that some would judge as appalling and go so far as to seek to cleanse society of such depraved animalistic atrocities and would go as far as to say, that the fall of the Roman Empire was based on such sexual debauchery."

"So where do we as a society draw the line?" Tangerine furthered her inquiries. "If molestation of children or even rape is subjectively okay, does that make it okay for the predator? And if so, what do we do with the victims?" Heat now began to filter into Tangerine's tone.

"Let me stop you there, Tangerine," Professor Patterson calmly spoke. "Your questions are great questions, but believe it or not, your questions are taking us into issues of morals and ethics. Rights and wrongs. In the field of psychotherapy, it's not about right and wrong but more of why and how; why do people behave or think or feel this way or that way and if impaired, how can we help them become unstuck. Remember, people don't seek help if they don't think they have a problem and it's not the role of the therapist to convince individuals they have a problem by projecting onto them values of right and wrong. So, let me ask you, Tangerine," Professor Patterson said, giving strong eye contact to her while now leaning against the edge of his desk. "If you, as a therapist, were given a client seeking help for his sexual bend towards children, how would you approach this individual?"

"I'd cut off his dick and shove it down his throat," Tangerine answered without thinking, sparking a laughing outburst throughout the room.

"Well then, maybe you're in the wrong field," Professor Patterson responded with what felt like towering superiority, reducing the laughter to a stilled seriousness. "Rule of thumb, if you desire to be a therapist, leave your values, prejudices, and judgments at the door in order to leave room for your client. If not, your counter-transferences will infringe and impede the therapeutic process that rightfully belongs to your client, regardless of why he or she has come to you."

Awkwardness befell the room. When Professor Patterson concluded, nothing was said. Even Tangerine's inflamed righteous indignation was squelched by the extinguishing power of Professor Patterson's words. He subjectively spoke a truth but objectively came across as a disciplinarian who hacked down the potential uprising of a student.

The long drawn out silence left the Professor to conclude that class was over, a therapeutic tool he has used in the classroom setting in the past. For the first time since the semester began, he released the students fifteen minutes before class was scheduled to end, this in lieu of the question and answer period. It was Professor Patterson's intention to have the students wrestle with their anxiety regarding the discussion left off between he and Tangerine. Issues of counter-transferences was a vital point he wanted them to get, beyond just the academic understanding. Empirical knowledge facilitated through experience, for this lesson, he knew, would be their best teacher. A cruel-to-be-kind way of educating.

The room of students dispersed with what felt like an atmosphere of somberness. Professor Patterson took his spot behind the desk and periodically glanced his way towards Tangerine's doings. Nothing out of the ordinary. She departed without a single hesitancy, leaving behind heightened feelings of foolishness in the pit of the Professor's stomach.

Halloween was approaching, bringing with it the soon-to-be time change. Summer's heat had vacated the atmosphere and allowed space for the dropped temperatures of fall to make their temporal residency. The sun shone but the earth was buffered by the fall's cool climate. Professor Patterson basked beneath the open, azure sky that displayed its vastness just above the collective leaves and branches of the Sycamore trees he laid beneath. He had already consumed his lunch and now laid still with mental meditations running rampant behind closed eyes. Thoughts of unwanted images of Tangerine danced in his head. The fantasy of courtship and all its entailing excitement infiltrated his mental reverie. Combating this invasive cognition seemed to be to no avail. Other thoughts were called upon to ward off the soliloquies of what he deemed stupidity and *stinking thinking*. Keeping her at bay with each passing effort and with each passing day was growing into utter futility. The more he tried to stop thinking about Tangerine, the more he seemed to ruminate about her. Control was being lost to the gripping clutches of desire. A lot in life Professor Patterson loathed, especially when the desire being unmet only perpetuated the suffering.

Tangerine and all the thoughts that tampered with her association led to a moment of self awareness. The Professor realized his own hypocrisy when discussing with the class about counter-transferences.

It was his own counter-transference that filled the room the moment he responded to Tangerine the way he did. His unmet expectations of unwanted desires came to the surface and fueled him to say what he said, initially thinking himself a good proctor but now thinking himself a hypocritical bastard. He had wronged her in front of her peers and sensed the guilt of his doings.

Somewhere during Professor Patterson's cerebral taunting, a voice spoke from above.

"Professor Patterson," a female spoke, causing the Professor to open his eyes to the vision of slight blurriness. "Sorry to disturb you, but I was hoping for a moment of your time."

After coming to with complete vision intact, to his wishful pleasant surprise, he beheld Tangerine standing over him. In a scurried fashion, he lifted his upper torso and situated himself in a seated position.

"Well, good afternoon, Tangerine. What can I do for you?"

"May I sit down, Professor Patterson?" Tangerine asked even though she foreknew that regardless of his answer, she was going to anyhow.

Tangerine's approaching of the Professor was her own volition. Lisa or Rimy were nowhere around, indicating no signs of some coercing through peer pressure or a dare. Tangerine had personal business to attend to with the Professor that needed to be done sooner rather than later.

"Yes, you may, but only on one condition."

"And what's that?"

"You call me, Gil."

"Fair enough, Gil." Although compliant, it felt awkward. Initially.

He didn't say it aloud, but he liked the way his name rolled off her tongue.

Tangerine seated herself on the grass near the Professor as he attempted to conceal the thrill he felt inside.

"What can I do for you, Tangerine?"

"I wanted to apologize for what happened in class today. I felt like I ruined the discussion by interjecting my projections, or as you put it, my counter-transferences that seemed to have gotten in the way. Then I thought about what you said regarding being in the wrong field and have been obsessing over it ever since, thinking maybe you're right. Maybe I am too judgmental to be a therapist? Here I thought I was pretty open minded only to embarrassingly discover how closed minded I really am. So Profess… Gil, I just wanted to say, I'm sorry and I'll try not to let it happen again, even with the few classes that remain."

The Professor sat attentively the whole time Tangerine was articulating her apology. Into one another's eyes they looked while she talked and he listened. Closely, he observed her and discovered she was much more beautiful then he thought her to be. Never had this much time been granted to look at her so deeply. Her fair pure skin. Her hazel-green eyes. Her perfectly shaped lips. Her lengthy black hair. Whatever desire he had for her before just got greater due to the chance he was now encountering.

"Tangerine," the Professor responded back without haste. "I wouldn't worry too much about whether you're in the right place or not. Your observations were right on the mark and your interjections are not one bit an infringement or interruption of the class. I encourage you to continue to inquire and speak your mind so freely. Mind speaking is such a rarity nowadays and I would expect no less from you. And though I thank you for the apology, it's not needed. You did nothing wrong and I hope with what little time we have left in the course, you would remain engaged and participate with your questions and comments."

"Either way, I think I just needed to get that off my chest. Gil, thanks for your time and for your kind assurance. And thanks for letting me interrupt your lunch. I would have asked after class, but I wasn't clear on my thinking until later and my obsessing about it wouldn't let me wait until the next class." Tangerine started to rise and be on her way as she said, "Again, thanks for your time and...I guess I'll see you in class."

Tangerine turned to walk away. Just then the Professor spoke up, "Tangerine."

She stopped and turned around, "Yes?" Her face presently out of the shade and in the spot light of the sun and Gil awed by this sight of a deeper radiant beauty Tangerine was now center staging.

"Are you heading somewhere important?"

"Not really."

"Somewhere you need to be?"

"No... not really, why?"

"Would you mind spending the rest of my lunch with me?" The Professor humbly asked, seeming to allow, for the first time in a long time, vulnerability to spill from his mouth and sounding more like a school boy asking a girl to go steady and not a man asking a woman to stay.

Initially taken back, Tangerine answered in the affirmative, "Yes."

Tangerine returned to her original position, this time with a welcoming smile from the Profess... from Gil. They spent Gil's remaining thirty minutes of lunch entwined in educational dialogue. Nothing deep and nothing to personal. But a shared moment in time that flew by way too fast. For the both of them. They consented to carry on the dialogue further the next time Tangerine felt inclined to share the shade with Gil; an inclination Gil hoped Tangerine would adhere to sooner rather than later.

7

...I'm getting tired of lying to your son, coming up with lame excuses for why you're not around and why you missed his graduation that he invited you to and desperately wanted you to attend. It hurt him that you weren't there, as it should and it should hurt you that he was hurt. There was a time when I felt sympathy for you and understood your reactive decision to have no initial contact with YOUR boy. But now, I'm starting to develop anger and disrespect towards you because of your irresponsibility and inexcusable neglecting of YOUR son. Just for your information, he wanted to write you another letter telling you about his graduation and the day spent, but I stopped him from doing it. Didn't want him to waste his time, telling him some BS that you were out of town and wouldn't be home to get his letter for some time. With the holidays coming, maybe you could find it in your stone heart to contact YOUR son and maybe I wouldn't have to keep lying to compensate for your neglecting of your responsibilities as a father.

Stella

"That was pretty blunt," Henry spoke for the first time after being handed the letter and reading it silently to himself. "I see she emphasized the word 'your.'"

"Attempting to get her point across you'd say," Gil retorted back.

"Why did I read this?" Henry asked.

Clearly understanding Henry's question due to the fact that Gil has never let Henry read any of the other many letters he has received pertaining to his son. "I don't know why," Gil answered. "Something inside me wanted to share this most recent letter with you and maybe because it's not from him."

"Do you get many letters like this from your sister-in-law?"

"Not this harsh. Most of the letters are from my son."

"Do you realize, Gil, in all our time spent, until this moment, you have never referred to the boy as your son."

"I know," Gil spoke through a voice of slight shame.

"Why tonight?"

"I don't know."

The two intellectual alpha-males sat together for a brief period of silence, Henry staring at Gil who was staring into a partially filled glass of beer.

"Is it Tangerine?" Henry asked.

"Is what Tangerine?"

"Is it time spent with her that's opening your heart unto new life?"

Henry was referring to the lunch periods that Gil and Tangerine shared a few times and its possible spawning of emotional effects it may be having on him.

"I'm not sure what it is, Henry. It could be my time with Tangerine. Let's not make it out to be more than what it is. We've only had a few lunch encounters. It hardly seems enough to qualify it as a catalyst for change."

"Hey, you're the psychologist. You should know the unpredictability of the psyche and the human creature. Nothing about human nature, human reaction, or human behavior can be accurately formatted. We're complicated creatures. Maybe the few encounters have been enough to crack you and now other human sentimentalities are starting to spill out. That's a good thing."

"Maybe," Gil spoke followed by a heavy sigh. "Whatever's happening to me, that which you define as good, I'm not sure I like it. First of all, Tangerine is basically forbidden fruit, no pun intended, and second, this child, …my son, well …how do I start being his father now after all these years of rejecting him and neglecting my parental responsibilities?"

"First off, this Tangerine girl is not forbidden…you're just scared. Once the semesters is over maybe you could risk taking it up a notch and asking her out to dinner or something simpler like meeting for coffee. Some quality alone time outside the school setting. As for your son, from what I gather, after all this time he still continues to reach out to you, seeming to so desperately want you, as his father, in his life. This child is starving for your fatherhood. Any little response from your end would fill his heart with more love and joy than you could even imagine. You and his relationship with you is all he hopes and dreams about. I know I'm conjecting, but I believe it to be true. The void of your absence is there but not truly actualized or felt because of the hopes and dreams of this child one day having his father. Not just any father…you. But let me say this, if you plan on making contact with this child, this son of yours, make sure you're going into it one hundred percent and not being an in-and-out of his life father figure. One step towards him on your part will cause him to leap into your arms and hold you without the possibility of letting go and losing you again whether figuratively or actually. Your commitment to him is for life. Remember that. Partial commitment would be the heartbreak of him and bring to the surface that void that is currently at bay. So before you make any hasty decision or impulsive move, you count the cost on this one. And another thing, don't try to make up for lost time, a fallacy people think they have the power to do. Start where you are and build from there. If you begin now, there are more years on the building end than there are on the neglected end. And one last thing, without the intent of putting pressure on you, time is running out and you know that. Soon, he will have to let you go if you don't show any interest on your part. So in this case, yes, time is of the essence."

Every word – conjecture or not - Henry spoke broadened the already deep gouge that Stella's letter authored.

"I just don't know if I'm ready for that kind of responsibility," Gil spoke with subtle sounds of sadness. "My heart doesn't seem to be in the right place."

"I'm not saying dive into this and wait for the emotions to follow the behavior. Just warm up to the possibility, and as you therapists would say, take baby steps."

The two professors concluded their night with another round and a different topic, purposely orchestrating the evening to end on a good note. Henry went to his nine o'clock appointment while Gil made his way home only to enter an empty, cold domain and struggle with a sleepless night of pervasive thinking of a child he was starting to see as his son.

While tossing beneath the blankets, Henry's words resonated in Gil's head. Henry was right and Gil knew it. Both about his fear of Tangerine and the commitment he would need to dedicate to his son if he so chose to travel down that road of reconciliation. The two persons of possibility scared the hell out of him. One required the aspects of romanticism and the other required the aspects of *agape* love, two components Gil knew he possessed at one time but now not sure if their dormant disposition over the many years had lead to a complete annihilation. Smart enough to know the intricate workings of the human makeup, he knew one would help determine the possibility of the other. If romanticism could be welled up to the surface, then the depth of committed nurturing love could be discovered beneath the hardened stone of his soul. One would be the foretelling of the possibility of the other. The contingent difference between the two is the given fact that he didn't know where Tangerine stood when it came to her feelings towards him. Accurately spoken by Henry, his son's intentions were very clear. Too painfully clear. Gil knew he could afford the risk of losing the possibility of courting Tangerine. The son, his son, couldn't be tested in the same like fashion. It was all or nothing. In completely or out completely, the latter state he has already been in for the last eight years. What happens with Tangerine may determine the outcome of what happens with his son. A cause and effect he was conjuring the strength to implement.

Henry had arrived ten minutes early. With his carnal blood boiling, his rational mind still contained some room to ponder the conversation he and his dear friend engaged in earlier that evening. Henry knew the truth he spoke was difficult for his friend to hear, but he had no regrets about saying it. It was in his friend's best interest to hear what needed to be said, even though Henry knew deep within the truth he spoke didn't come from an attempt to pretend to understand what Gil was going through. There are some shoes that Gil has walked in that Henry has never had to wear, one pair being deeply in love and losing that love to the fate of death. The other pair, having a child. Henry, being a Cultural Anthropologist, never believed the human creature was designed nor should be bound to the man-made modality of monogamy. This premise was made clear in his doctoral dissertation on the parallels and influences of religious monotheism and relational monogamy, which became published and highly controversial. By no means did this conclude that Henry was polytheistic in his religious beliefs but certainly a proponent of polyamorous relationships. Although married, for completely different reasons than the reasons the masses married for, Henry's polyamorous propensity was powerful enough to navigate an open lifestyle that did not include faithfulness or the procreating of another, a standard Henry's wife was well aware of and openly accepted before she said "I do." This meant that the truth Henry had said to his dear friend came from the cognitive womb of understanding and not the empathetic cradle of the heart.

It was Henry's anthropological paradigm that gave him freedom from guilt to act out his primal desires. Studying abroad throughout his life and encountering the many different beliefs and rituals of other people and other cultures enlightened him to the vast array of human nature. This being so, Henry practiced and preached that human primordial nature – the reptilian brain - should not be repressed or condemned because of civil progress. Natural man was made by the hands of a higher deity and fashioned in a way that social evolution has and was further destroying. Maxims of morality were the poisons of natural disintegration according to Henry and he sought to live in a way that gave him liberty to gratify instinctual wantings without hesitancy or remorse. Pleasure and pain being the two primordial hubs he enjoyed tantalizing.

Two minutes to nine. Henry vacated the vehicle and headed towards room 22 at the Travel Lodge. Even before meeting with Gil, his appointment with the Black Magic Woman had been prearranged. The usual place at the usual time. A protocol established after a few months of customer-regularity.

With two fifty in cash and a pulsating libido, Henry ascended the steps that lead to his awaited chamber of permissible delights. Soon, just steps away, the tight, young body of a beautiful vixen adorned in leather and lace, equipped with her arson of pleasure -whip, hot wax, and leash – known as The Black Magic Woman, AKA Lisa Richardson, was ready to give Henry more than his money's worth.

Nearly a year ago, Henry responded to the enticing offer advertised in the *LA Weekly* of what The Black Magic Woman would do for the right price. In turn, nothing about the advertisement was false. In fact, the service rendered and the one rendering it was more than Henry expected. So much more that Henry evolved into a regular. A twice-a-monther.

It was only after unexpectedly crossing paths on the college campus with the dark, female villain dressed in her civilian attire did Henry come in contact with The Black Magic Woman's true identity. They both responded with surprise and rightful acknowledgments of who the other was. He, Henry, the professor of Cultural Anthropology; she, Lisa Richardson, a student of psychology. Fortunately, their first time encounter on the campus was without the accompaniment of others, granting them a golden opportunity to handle the given dilemma with maturity and to design a plan that they would continue in their purchased dynamic while guaranteeing one another anonymity. They did so while maintaining the appearance of professor and student simply talking. Since then, their charade has been stringently upheld. Their private pleasures have not once spilled into their professional personas. Luckily, Lisa's major has kept her away from ever being one of Henry's students, although she has joked about taking one of his courses during a few of their post-sexual liaison conversations.

The knowing of one another's true identity seemed to have never infringed on their business at hand. It seemed to, in fact, enhance the experience. For the both of them. Each flourished in their provider-consumer roles and even reenactments of student-teacher dynamics were played out. She, the struggling student, and he, the teacher willing to grant extra tutoring for her after class. She, getting spanked for wrong answers, and he, receiving services of gratitude for assisting her with her education.

Nothing about their liaisons were predetermined. Some nights, she was the sadist. Others, she was the masochist. Either way, Henry got off and that was the product he was purchasing. Once the 'getting off' was completed, unlike other clientele, Henry stuck around and spent some post-time with The Black Magic Woman who would morph back into Lisa Richardson. The two would talk as one human being to another about topics that had nothing to do with the animalistic act they had just committed. A kind of friendship had developed that was reciprocated with equality, or at best, mutuality. A friendship only defined within the parameters of their hotel domain. Yet, if ever, to be spilled outside of their purchased space.

Inevitably, they would come in unexpected contact during campus crossings, making eye acknowledgements of one another whenever either one was in the company of others. When traversing mutually solo, they would stop and briefly chat, even arrange for an encounter, which Lisa had come to make Henry a priority when it came to reservations. This priority making of Lisa's for Henry was not only for economical profit, but also on her developed liking for him as a person. It all seemed very arousing for both of them to have a secret contact that no one knew about; a guilty pleasure of sorts - minus the guilt. Not even Tangerine nor Gil, confidants of Lisa and Henry were made aware of the secret truth that lurked beneath their noses.

Only the burning wicks from the candlesticks housed in the candelabra that rested securely on top of the hotel TV gave off light in the squared structure of room 22. The intent was an ethereal ambiance flared with overtones of a macabre setting. The layout was Henry's request, hoping to experience the stepping into a medieval dungeon feel with the anticipation of torture by the menacing hands of his hired leather and laced dungeon master. Henry, the convict, was ascribed guilty for lascivious acts, like that of the Marquis De Sade, and was now to bear his sentence at the free lancing plans of punishment by his subleased Dominatrix. Tonight, Henry would receive his just punishment and love every painful moment.

Strapped to the corners of the bed's footposts like one tied to a rack, Henry laid helplessly and submissively on his back, awaiting the lashings that were rightfully due. The dark, curvaceous figure paced slowly around the bed, periodically striking the exposed body of the bound prisoner and leaving red welts as images of enforced Talion

Law. Grimacing beneath each scolding lambaste, heightened sensations of sexual ecstasy coursed through the prey's anatomy like charges of electricity, sending the body into an arching-squirming display of reactionary splendor.

Flogging her victim with what she deemed as just the right amount of slashing force, each one with pleasurable intent, she moved on to the next medium of choice in order to ascend her convict to the next threshold of arousal. The small hands of one determined to painfully please the sprawled out Henry who nonverbally begged for more removed two of the burning candles from the candelabra. The Black Magic Woman with cat-like agility sprang and mounted Henry's restricted body without losing a single drop of the hot wax formed atop of each candlestick. With a no-holds-bar, the nocturnal siren peered deeply into Henry's eyes as she slowly brought the two burning flames together for the near emergence of the flames into one combined fire. Just inches away from touching one another and several inches above Henry's exposed vulnerable chest, she proceeded to slowly tip the candles inward with flames soon to intertwine as one, prefixed by the descending drops of hot wax falling and searing the skin of Henry's bare chest. Wax continued to melt, providing the leathered and laced sadist with more drops of bewitching delight that she trailed from the chest to just above the hardened phallic, making quite certain that no liquid outside of human saliva dare touch the erected idol.

Through bright red, puckered lips, air was exhaled to extinguish the flames. Excess liquefied wax and the charred wicks were daggered into each of Henry's nipples like two cigars being smoldered out, accompanied by the sounds of agonizing delight catapulting from Henry's mouth. The tenebrous goddess then flung her weapons of pouring and searing pleasantries with aggressive intent out away from each side of the bed and littered them somewhere in the confines of the darkened room.

The die was cast and The Black Magic Woman's incantation was having its way. Henry's body was surged with unbridled euphoria as he danced on the thin line between pleasure and pain. The enchanting fem-daredevil of the night was ruling with her spellbinding powers and was now prepared to obliterate her prey with a climactic blow.

Henry was nearing his breaking point. A release was inevitable. With a few ups and downs of hand and mouth in rhythmic harmony, it was all over. Henry's literal climax was the conclusion he had arranged and paid for. All else was elaborate foreplay.

The night surpassed his phantasmal expectations and the extra fifty dollars economically displayed his appreciation, which was initially met with resistance but soon gave way to acceptance.

The two regressed back into their roles of reality and enjoyed one another's authentic human company. Henry, still completely nude, but now untied, relished in a state of utter contentment while Lisa, adorned in casual garments without any exposure of any private parts, rested her hard worked body, belly down, alongside Henry. Neither one was pressed for time. So, they shared the next several minutes communicating on a decorous level in the after glow of primordial satisfaction.

"I think, Henry," Lisa said, before inhaling a drag from the cigarette her and Henry shared, both displaying their disregard for the hotel's no smoking policy. "And don't repeat me on this, I have a strong hunch that my good friend, Tangerine, has a thing for your friend, Gil."

A few months after Lisa and Henry's unexpected quad encounter on the school campus, when they genuinely experienced how small the world really is, did she also learn that Henry and one of her professors, Professor Patterson, were good friends.

"Is that so? And what makes you suspect such likings?"

"His name seems to be brought up by her often and she has sat with him at lunch a few times. And I can just tell. Call it woman's intuition."

"So, she has never come straight out and told you she has a thing for Professor Patterson?" Henry inquired with the intent of gathering hard evidence for his friend, Gil.

"She doesn't have to. I can just tell. And what about Professor Patterson, has he ever said anything about her?"

"Only mentioned the uniqueness of her name," Henry told her with the knowledge that his good friend had a deep liking for Tangerine but wasn't about to break his friend's confidentiality in the act of collaborative Cupiding.

"I keep telling her that she wants to fuck him, which she denies. I'm also suspicious of Professor Patterson. I get a feel that he has an attraction towards her. He seems a bit different lately. Like he's nicer or something…softer. Not so much the prick that he is. I've actually seen him smile in our last few classes. I've even caught him a few times looking towards Tangerine and I as we were getting our stuff ready to leave after class. He's never looked up from his desk after class. As he's never looked up from a role call until the time he called out Tangerine's name. Not only did he look up, it was like he fell into some kind of temporary trance. It was a strange moment. The whole class felt it. I sure did. You're telling me, Henry, that Professor Patterson hasn't said anything beyond the mentioning of her name?"

"Nothing, sweetheart. Just the uniqueness of her name."

"I find that hard to believe," Lisa stated with confidence as she glared at Henry with investigative eyes.

Henry felt her stare but did not glance her way. There was no breaking him. "You can peer all you want," Henry spoke, addressing Lisa's stare without turning towards her. "But you're not going to find anything other than what I told you. There's nothing more to tell."

And to his guns, Henry stuck. Lisa was persistent, but to no avail. The subject was quickly dropped and, in turn, their evening came to an end. Henry gathered his belongings, gave Lisa her well-earned monetary reward, squeezed her with a warm 'see-ya-real-soon' embrace, and left the room well ahead of Lisa's departure to head back home to his domesticated life and his domesticated wife.

Lisa lingered a bit and briefly sought to analyze Henry's affect when he spoke of the dynamic, or the lack there of, of Tangerine and Professor Patterson. Attempting to use her novice psychology skills, no insight surfaced. Maybe Henry was telling the truth and she figured to leave it at just that.

However, there was an insight that did surface during her analytical reverie and the use of psychological tools came in handy in assisting her with defining the serendipitous phenomenon that unexpectedly came. It was she who really wanted to fuck Professor Patterson, and this whole time, she had been projecting that desire unto Tangerine, falsely using her as the scapegoat of her own repressed feelings. And if that diagnosis were true, maybe she was also projecting a story of relational possibility between Tangerine and the Professor that was really occurring in her subconscious yearnings, compelled by a fixated Electra Complex she had towards Professor Patterson.

The more she sought for answers, the more questions were asked. It was all too much for one night. She used the tool of sublimation and gathered her gear and exited the premises. There's a fine line between self-actualization and self-fulfilling prophecy, and Lisa wasn't prepared to walk it. At least not tonight. Not alone in room 22.

Dear dad…

Love,

your son.

8

"Once you have completed your test," Professor Patterson declared while handing out the final exam to each student. "Place the scantron and your final paper face down next to one another on my desk and the exam face up next to either the scantron or your paper. Basically, follow the lead of the first student's placement. You have the whole period to complete the exam, and once you're done, you're free to leave. Best of luck." Upon returning to his desk, Professor Patterson turned around and said, "You may begin."

Anxious students frantically turned their final exam over and plunged into the fifty multiple-choice questions placed before them. Questions ranging from defining various modalities to diagnosing disorders. Pressured by the fact that 40% of their grade depended on the results of the exam.

The room fell into a concentrated silence with periodic sounds of pages turning. Professor Patterson, the calmest in the room, was busy surfing the web for miscellaneous information. Basically, being as productive as possible while simultaneously killing time. Not once did he peer up to investigate the possibility of cheaters. Such things were of no concern for him. He was a professor, not an enforcer of rules. A cheater only cheats him or herself was his philosophy. One which made teaching that much easier for him and that much more enjoyable.

Minutes began passing after the initial hour. The first student arose to perform the protocol mentioned by Professor Patterson at the beginning of the class and set the placement standard for all those that followed. The student whispered to the Professor for some clarity on where exactly to place the required paperwork. Directed by the Professor's pointing finger, the student set the standard by placing his scantron and final essay paper face down in two separate places and his exam questions face up in a third column. Not long after the first did other students exhibit their completion of the exam. A little over half the class had finished the exam and left the room. The others still had about forty minutes before time ran out. One of those left behind was Tangerine. Lisa had already departed with the earlier birds.

With three minutes left before time was up, two students remained. Nearly a minute later, one of the two got up and completed the mode of operation, leaving the remaining student alone with the Professor and two final minutes to go. To the Professor's surprise, the last to finish the exam was Tangerine, not one the Professor would suspect to have encountered difficulty with the exam.

"And the last shall be first," the Professor stated aloud, broking the silence in an attempt to lighten the mood with some jovial interplay. "Time's up, Tangerine." He stated after first checking his watch.

"No problem, Professor Patterson," Tangerine spoke using the formal name of Gil within this setting without exposing the fact that she had actually been done for about thirty minutes now. Her intent was to linger around and try to get some alone time with the Profess... Gil. "I'm finished."

It didn't dawn on him until she approached his desk to turn in her papers that he was alone with her for the first time in the classroom setting. The thought sparked nervousness and a possible opportunity to initiate Henry's advice and ask her out for dinner or just coffee, now that she seemed to have completed all the qualifications that qualified her as a *past* student, at least for this class.

"Profess... ." Tangerine tried to speak.

"Tangeri… ." Gil spoke at the same time Tangerine spoke, he interrupting her and she interrupting him. "You first, Tangerine."

"I just wanted to say," Tangerine attempting to carry on where she got cut off. "I've really enjoyed your course and definitely have plans to take some more with you in the future."

"I'm glad to hear of both – the enjoying of the current course and your plans for future involvement with other courses," Gil responded while concealing the inner tension of wanting her physical proximity in future classes of his and never wanting her to be his student again. "It'll be nice, as it was throughout this course, having you in some of my other classes. Your presence has been a benefit to me and I look forward to more encounters in the near future. And hey, just because after today you may not be my student anytime soon doesn't mean you can't approach me and join me for lunch beneath the trees. Of course, only if you want to."

"I like that idea. I think I'll be taking you up on your offer sometime."

"That'll be great. I'd like that."

"Well, …I guess I'll be going. Again, Professor Patterson, thanks for everything."

"You're very welcome Tangerine. Very welcome. Take care."

"You too," was the last thing she said before turning to leave the room.

An inner gnawing voice screamed for immediate action. To stop her and say what needed to be said before the golden moment was blown.

"Tangerine," Gil spoke, projecting his voice just before she completed her exit out the door.

"Yes, professor?"

"Could you come here, please?"

"Sure."

He watched her as she returned into the area where he didn't have to project his voice and proceeded to ask, "I was wondering, if maybe you had some free time on your hands…if you'd like to get together sometime, preferably outside of school for some dinner or simply some coffee?" The nerves and rapid heartbeat being concealed by the articulation of his thoughts and his collective mannerism.

Without a moment of hesitancy, Tangerine responded by saying, "Yes, I would like that very much. And I would like that sooner rather than later."

"How about this evening?" Gil inquired, indirectly showing off his spontaneity, in essence, his impulsivity.

"How about now?" Tangerine answered with a question, returning a demonstration of her greater level of spontaneity.

"How about giving me about an hour so I can organize these papers. Let's say one thirty we meet at Kailua Java?"

"One thirty, it is."

"I assume you know where Kailua Java is?"

"You assume right. I will seen you then."

"Yes, you will."

They simultaneously had child-like grins as they gazed a little deeper in to one another, sharing non-verbally their mutual excitement for what serendipitously just transpired. Tangerine about-faced and migrated towards her departure as Gil watched her exit and vanish out the classroom door. Boyish fever raced through his body as he thought about what just happened in mild disbelief.

Tangerine had caught up with Lisa and discussed their speculations on how they did on the exam. Lisa had invited Tangerine to join her and Rimy for some post-exam celebratory drinks, but Tangerine informed her that she had a prior engagement, choosing not to mention with whom. This wasn't a ploy to keep it secret or protect Professor Patterson. Tangerine just wasn't in the mood to hear Lisa's possible adolescent shit.

Lisa, disappointed but not angered, went her way, while in return, Tangerine killed the time on her hands by browsing and window shopping. Nothing purchased. Just a whole lot of looking.

She'd arrived ten minutes prior to the established time. With a chi-tea and a nervous disposition, she procured the most secluded seats in the establishment. This she did to provide her and Gil with some kind of visual autonomy and social segregation in order to interact with unbridled words without the overspill of dialogue falling into neighboring ears.

There was something strange and uncertain about the soon-to-be meeting with the Profess…Gil outside of school grounds. Strange and uncertain but not "impairing" as Gil may phrase it. Tangerine had daydreamed numerous encounters of this type with Gil outside of the campus setting, although she never imagined it coming to fruition and if ever, certainly not this soon. Always seeming to be fortified with a sense of self-agency, Tangerine welcomed serendipitous spontaneity and was willing and ready to relish in the unexpected granted opportunity of her phantasmal muses around Gil to become incarnate.

Just prior to leaving her car and entering the coffee shop, Tangerine had refreshed herself with reapplied lipstick and a single spray of perfume. Not much was needed to enhance the God-given beauty that Tangerine brought with her when delivered into the world. A beauty that she confidently embraced and a beauty that instilled fear into the male species and envy into the female gender. And Gil was no exception. Tangerine scared the hell out of him.

Five minutes late Gil arrived with his day's attire and an additive deep brown leather coat accompanied with an apology. He was greeted with a warm smile and forgiveness for his tardiness.

The two sat in their con-joint seclusion and soon found solace for each of their unspoken anxiousness in gleaming countenances and dangling conversation. The natural progression of deeper dialogue was subtle, having its way through the broaching of topics with direct yet not intrusive questions.

"Tangerine," Gil spoke after much time had already elapsed since his late arrival. "And I know I'm asking the question you've probably heard throughout your life… ."

"My name," Tangerine interrupted with her rhetorical statement, aware of the elephant that has traveled with her throughout her life.

"Yes, your name," Gil calmly replied back.

"Both of my parents are a bit eccentric. They both grew up in the seventies. Free love, Woodstock, Civil Rights movement, Vietnam protestors. You name it from that era of time, they did it. On top of their liberal pattern of thought, …oh, did I mention they were philosophy and biology grads from Berkley? A little more seasoning flare to their already-out-there ways. My mother's family history traces back to Bohemia, a birthright she embraced and a lifestyle she practiced. Be patient with me, Gil," she said, calling him by his first name, something they re-established after she had called him Professor Patterson when he first arrived following her 'hello.' "There's a few more ingredients to this recipe. My mother always sought to be unique. Uniquely different. Uniquely creative. Uniquely crazy," she sarcastically stated followed by a harmless smirk. "My mother, who still fervently paints today, always incorporates the color orange in her paintings, a trademark of her artistry, being that orange had always been her favorite color since she was a child. And since orange would be a strange name for a child, as though Tangerine isn't, she thought the next best closest thing…or should I say, the next shade of orange would be Tangerine. So…after convincing my father of the name, they both agreed, - with excessive persistency on my mother's part - that their first and only daughter would be called Tangerine. And due to the fact that anything attached to the name would possibly corrupt the natural beauty of such a name, my birth certificate came without a last name. Only Tangerine. Now, twenty-two years later, my mother continues to remind me that the name is symbolic for what she deems to be her favorite thing in the whole wide world, her daughter, Tangerine."

Gil sat enthralled providing her with undivided attention, watching this, only hours ago, former and possibly soon-to-be again student of his, who was half his age, unfold before his eyes. Staring at her in the context of this intimate setting elicited his vision to see with unimpeded clarity. Their previous interactions weren't as personal, intense nor this transparent. There was something sacred here, something to be deeply valued. A magnetism that went beyond Tangerine's looks. And yet, there was a profanity easing its way in. A creeping backlashing of sorts Gil began to encounter from within due to the delving into this level of closeness. Tangerine's God-scripted belle reflected his own facial imperfection, like holiness exposing sin, her illuminance darkened his maimed shadow and triggering a self-consciousness that hadn't been experienced in years. While listening to her, inside he wrestled diligently with insecurities and the debilitating fact that she stared directly into the mangled portion of his anatomy that, no matter what he did, *it* could neither be hidden nor denied. Repressed memories and visceral moments from childhood bullies that constantly ridiculed him for his God-given defect were emerging to the surface. The amygdala was coming on line and his central-nervous system was ramping up. Fight, flight or freeze were becoming the delegated options of choice. He contended like mad to maintain his composure and get back to the experience at hand. To keep the higher-executive portion of his brain ruling. To no avail. The effects of such inner conflict and menacing inferiority were beginning to manifest in his behavior. His piercing eye contact was waning. Sporadic turnings of his head began to occur that wasn't there before, looking around the room as though he was looking for someone or something when in fact he was attempting to look away from Tangerine. Unaware of his actions, he was unconsciously attempting to give Tangerine the good side of his face as to protect her from having to visually encounter his grotesqueness, a sight she had looked upon for over nine weeks now, and a truth Gil was incapable of ascertaining in his time of need. And due to this inner civil war that Gil was battling, he had no verbal response to Tangerine's explanation of the genesis of her name; an explanation she provided to the very question he posed.

For Tangerine, Gil's sudden behavior came across as a losing of interest in their time together. He appeared to have mentally and emotionally checked out.

Not one given to pseudo anything, Tangerine accepted the fact that their time together seemed to have run its course, she taking this cue from Gil's display of indifference.

It had tipped over in to an over stayed welcome.

It was time to go.

"I'm sorry to cut this off," Tangerine spoke as she broke the obtrusive dangling silence. "But I'm supposed to meet up with some friends later… you know… celebration for ending the semester."

"Oh…of course," Gil responded, unaware of the condoning of her lie. "I understand."

Tangerine quickly arose from her chair and reached out her hand towards Gil to conclude the night on a conventional handshake and stated, "Professor Patterson," regressing back to a reactive formality. "Thanks for taking time away from your busy schedule and sharing coffee with me. Maybe we'll see one another on campus or the next time I take another one of your courses."

Tangerine released her firm grip and made her way towards the entrance door. Before having a chance to regroup his befuddled mind, she was gone. Only then did the impeding feelings of inferiority and semi-dissociative state vanish, returning the rational brain back to its operational capacity to know that something clearly went awry as a lingering sourness filled the air. He quickly turned to catch her and simply say goodbye but Tangerine was out the door and long gone.

Gathering his bearings, Gil knew he had blown it. The ghostly relics of the past had made their presence known and infiltrated what golden chance had given him in real time. Fate was kind enough to supply him with an open window of opportunity that suddenly closed due to his fallacy of belief. Now *it* and she were gone, without the ability to fix the immediacy of the moment. It was lost and he damned himself for it. Even if he conjured up the courage to be vulnerably honest with her, telling her of his feelings of hideousness in the presence of her flawless beauty, he couldn't. There was no way of getting in touch with her, no bridge-of-contact for him to cross. It was burned the moment Tangerine walked away and stepped out the door.

Gil sat, feeling lonely for the first time in years. The cocoon of being comfortably numb manifested a crack. The elated emotions of temporal companionship with Tangerine created a cleft that came with the consequential price of emptiness. Saying "yes" to her invite-for-connection set him up to toy with the double-edge sword of intimacy that ended with him being cut wide open. His initial boyish excitement and rejuvenated manhood were cut asunder by an abrupt ending that left him in a state of implosive aching and self-loathing. And although wounded by the unexpected contamination of their enchanted togetherness and feeling helplessly subjugated to the mastery of his inflamed emotions, he wanted her back and already missed her.

9

'Twas the season to be jolly' time of the year that recently descended upon the Western Land of Liberty. Peace on Earth and mercy mild fallaciously lingered in the air as the madness for parking and purchasing joy-killed any possibility for an authentic Christmas spirit. The gracious givers of gifts were frantically seeking the right item to give to loved ones that would possibly convey their message of love during this time of giving, possibly minimizing, even obliterating all altruistic intentions. Consumerism-with-us was the Emmanuel of the American Christmas. Old Saint Nick wore cash-green while Dasher, Dancer, Prancer and Rudolph had been replaced by the reindeers of American Express, Visa and MasterCard that guided parental sleighs tonight.

And as cynical as one may be to the fabricated jolliness of a Capitalistic Christmas, some facts couldn't be denied. Patience seemed a little longer. Tolerance, a bit more. Gratitude deeper. Strangers friendlier. Love possibly stronger. And for the briefest moment, the illusion of the possibility of peace on Earth was actually believable. Maybe the real Emmanuel - the God-with-us - did revisit the Earth in the month of December to inspire the human creature's heart to believe, if, for a moment, that Heaven and Nature could sing as one and a Joy To The World genuinely could be experienced through a power from above transmitted through human's below.

Gil didn't have any regard for the high American holidays. He'd preferred the month of December to be removed from the calendar altogether. Family and the gathering of loved ones was no longer an attribute that made up his holidays. Aloneness and reclusion defined his Decembers and the waiting out of those long drawn out thirty-one days that seemed to crawl like a snail up a hill. Although offered to partake in Christmas gatherings and dinners by in-laws and colleagues, Gil politely declined and opted for seclusion and temporal hibernation.

It wasn't always as such for Gil. There was a period when Christmas was the most wonderful time of the year. Tinsel, eggnog, mistletoe, and a big tall Oh-Christman-Tree-Oh-Chritmans-Tree were the holiday condiments of his life, beginning in the latter part of November and carrying on through until the first part of January. Gil and his wife at the time compelled by equal enthusiasm sought to decorate their humble abode with a different theme each year. They also highly enjoyed the gathering of family and friends, welcoming them all with love and open arms and even established a yearly ritual to invite students who had nowhere to go for the holidays. Their hospitality was second to none and all felt the deep pangs when it all came to an unexpected but understanding end eight years ago.

Their last Christmas together, Gil and his now deceased wife, just two months before their first-born was due, came up with the idea of a baby theme for that year's Christmas. Baby blue would be the dominant holiday color strewn throughout the house. Baby blue socks hung like bulbs amid the branches of the Christmas tree, baby blue material draped the tree like garland, and the angel perched atop the tree harkened the herald horn in a baby blue robe. There was nothing in the house that final Christmas that didn't say a boy was on his way; not the Messianic-Boy of Nazareth but their baby boy who would change the lives of the Patterson's forever.

Not the *change* they had expected; nor the one they had hoped for.

Since that final baby-blue-Christmas, no tree, no tinsel, no reef, and certainly no holiday cheer has set foot in that house that once facilitated the true spirit of giving. The relics of a love-filled-jolly past had been stuffed in a box and put away in the darkened attic of yesterdays with the angered, bitter and grieving intentions to never return.

The only companions Gil had during his month of isolation was last semester's former students' papers he read and graded, accompanied by a bottle of wine and tracks of Dylan to accompany his misery. Even his Tuesday evening regimented meetings with Henry were infringed upon during December and placed on hold until after the first of the year, due to Henry traveling back East for time with his family.

However, there was another who seemed to be making her way into Gil's cave of alienation during this holiday break. An intruder that constantly broke into his brain and ransacked his thinking. With all his rational might and intellectual fortitude, he fought to keep the pestering break-ins from occurring and reoccurring. Nothing seemed to work. Tangerine's image and the haunting remembrance of their last encounter that ended on such a bad note were obsessively ruminating in his head. The recollection of her face that he attentively gazed upon during their conversations perpetuated his attraction towards her and the unrelenting desire to see her again.

Reenactments played out in his mind's-eye on how he would have handled the situation differently. He thought of that moment when the awkwardness had occurred. He thought of how he would have intervened in attempts to preserve the pleasure of one another's company before it took a sudden turn for the worse. He thought of his foolery. He thought of his insecurity. He thought of his immaturity. He thought and he thought until his acute thinking became a static condition.

An obsession.

The gnawing feelings of helplessness plagued him. All the 'what ifs' or 'should ofs' only cut the wound deeper due to the fact that they couldn't be actualized. Remedied. The real Tangerine was nowhere to be found while the imaginative Tangerine, unwanted and going nowhere, was an antagonist of unmet desires that only served to torture and exasperate his wish for another chance.

Gil had tasted the delightful fruit of Tangerine and consequentially lost his paradise of numbing bliss. One bite was all it took for his fall to happen and she too beguiled him unto a psychic infirmity that knew no relief. Only now, feeling emotionally naked and deeply panged by the beckoning of those unmet desires, did he regret not heeding the warnings of tampering with the luring power of the laws of attraction.

Permissible vestiges of her and wonderings of her doings and whereabouts made his nights of repose nearly impossible. Reading a novel as a medium of sanctity and distraction only proved futile. Getting through pages and having no recollection of what was read served as a reminder that the more he tried to vanquish Tangerine from his thinking, the more she occupied and dominated his mental space.

She had become an unwanted guest that he paradoxically wanted more and more.

Having for sometime now put off his responsibilities and his ascetic 'doings' during his darkened Decembers – (that of grading papers) - he was sparked by the charge of hope when considering a comforting thought. Reading Tangerine's essay. Gil considered the possibility of her visceral companionship through the reading of her written words and the inner workings of her mind unfolded on paper. Gil also considered how crazy and childish he was starting to think and soon to behave. To do such an act with full awareness of his intentions was in fact an act of regression. To think, feel, believe he could somehow conjure up the presence of her spirit through the incantation of reading words was for him a willful move towards lunacy. Clearly the fruit of entangled bedazzlement was weakening more and more the stoic warrior who showed symptoms of surrender by willingly laying down his shield of detachment and willingly descending swiftly in to the abyss of make-believe.

And so, the spell was cast as the idea came to fruition.

10

Gil poured himself a glass of wine and picked through the stack of essays, bypassing all the other students in a quest to find Tangerines. *Body Dismorphic; The Cultural Conditioned Disorder* was the title of Tangerine's paper. In the syllabus and clarified in class, the student's final essay assignment was to pick a disorder from the Diagnostic and Statistical Manual for disorders-IV and write a ten page paper that entailed the disorders symptoms, etiological possibilities, and a section for personal reaction to the disorder and it's impact on or experience within the student's life.

Ascetically, he read through the first parts, valuing her opinions but considering them elementary while restraining his compelling anxiousness to get to the personal portion of her work. There is where he figured he would find companionship by proxy.

And more than he had bargained for.

Tangerine, in the personal section of the essay, spoke about her father and the real disfigurement he lived with each and everyday of his life. The same disfigurement she'd looked upon since birth. It was a comparative piece, showing how contrasting and how unfortunate it was that her father, who's dismorphed face was real and yet, he existed with vigor and vitality, whereas others, whose faces in comparison were made up of perfection could view themselves as some kind of Quasimodo and be psychologically and emotionally impaired through such cognitive distortions. She went on to say that growing up with her father's facial wound conditioned her to see beyond the surface to the beauty that laid within and deemed her father, regardless of what others might have thought, as the most handsome man alive and would have him no other way.

Upon finishing the paper, Gil instantly thought of his eye and his own facial disfigurement. Call it deprivation. Call it desperation. Gil felt like Tangerine was conveying an indirect message to him. As though she was saying to him that his lazy left eye was unnoticeable to her and regardless of his imperfection, she saw him as attractive.

Such thinking, delusional or not, shot an adrenaline of rejuvenating hope through him with reactive physiology that curbed the longing and remorse he had been roaming with since the holiday break; more specifically, since the injurious crime at the coffee establishment he was culpable of. In that split second, the impossible seemed possible. The beauty and the beast were not separated by such an extraordinary chasm. Tangerine's ability to 'see beyond' was the indemnifying contingency for an egalitarian relationship between he and her. This was the schematic thinking that, even if for a short duration of time, absolved his fallen condition.

With his bolted resurgence came a clarity of thinking and a wild possibility. It dawned on him following the breaking up of muddled mental fog that there might just have been an attempted reaching out on Tangerine's part since their encounter and its dreadful conclusion at the coffee house. He also knew this idea was a deeper sinking in to wishful thinking but also knew he had nothing to lose and possibly redemption to gain.

Gil established at the onset of each class he taught that if any student needed to contact him outside of the class room setting for reasons whatsoever, he was available via e-mail at Gil419@----------.---, an address written on the board the first day of each semester. However, rarely did he check his e-mail and more rarely did he ever respond. Just a few more attributes that confirmed why students considered him an asshole.

Compelled to do what he rarely, again, if ever, did, he logged on and checked his e-mail with the belief that maybe, just miraculously maybe, Tangerine sought to communicate with him in a way that went beyond student-teacher dynamic. The digital modem couldn't work fast enough. But it worked and he was in. Inbox **(75)** unread messages. One click away and his preconceived notions would be either confirmed or denied. Hypothesis true or null and void. He clicked. Addresses revealed themselves. All seventy-five. Although not certain of what he was searching for, any possible connection tied to the word Tangerine must correlate to her, so he theorized. Scrolling down, he bypassed all mail that had no alluding to her distinct name with the hopes he wouldn't have to go back and methodically decode indirect possibilities. And there it was. Clear as day. Tangerine85@-----.---. Three quarters of the way down. After a quick calculation, the 85 he figured to be the year of her birth. Another quick calculation and he concretely encountered the discrepancy of their ages. He knew it existed but was now seeing the hard fact of the matter, a fact that confirmed another possible truth he held; he was old enough to be her father.

Once more, he clicked. Sprawled before his eyes was a lengthy e-mail dated the day after their meeting. Scripted at about 2:00 a.m.

Dear Gil,

It is about two in the morning and I can't sleep. I am too ill-at ease. It's been about twenty-four hours since we met for coffee and I haven't stopped thinking about how things turned out – whether you are aware of it or not. I'm quite sure you must have noticed my sudden change followed by my abrupt leaving. I lied to you about meeting others and having to go for that reason. I'm sorry for lying to you Gil. The truth – I was offended by what I perceived as you suddenly becoming bored and looking like you mentally took off elsewhere. I felt rejected and I don't do well with rejection. So I impulsively did what I usually do when rejected, I take flight. Immature, I know. I'm working on it. So I left and conjured up a lie to justify my immature leaving. Again, sorry. But if you were getting bored or tired of our time together, you should have just come right out and told me. Believe it or not, Gil, I am a big girl and can handle the truth – even though I lied. I thought we were getting along. I know I was deeply enjoying our time together.

Anyway, I'm sure I've taken enough of your time already so I won't keep you. I guess I needed to get this off of my chest since it's been eating away at me since I left the coffee shop. Whatever it means, thank you for our time spent – which I thoroughly enjoyed – and I guess I will see you around the campus after the holidays.

Tangerine.
P.S. Merry Christmas

Gil read the e-mail twice. He could hear Tangerine's voice speak through her written words, much more intimately and personally than he heard through her essay paper. Although the message wasn't leaning towards the positive, the fact that she exhibited mild symptoms of obsession over what occurred between them and reached out to convey her feelings to him was complimentary. It also served to normalize his obsessive state that he had been bogged down with since.

Time had already been lost due to his indifference towards the modern era of communication, via e-mail. Nearly two weeks had passed since Tangerine sought refuge through confessing herself to him and, with what he assumed, an underlying desire for a response. Without furthering the already delayed response, Gil clicked on reply and scripted his take on things.

Dear Tangerine,

It is not my habit to check my emails. I usually don't. But I was compelled to this evening and I came across yours. This is my truthful excuse why it's taken so long to respond back to you, although you didn't necessarily ask for a reply. I took the liberty to give you a reply. Because of my lack or disregard for talking through a computer, I would like to talk to you by phone and explain what happened to me that day during our time together at the coffee house. So if you would please, call me as soon as you get this – regardless of the time. I'll be expecting your call – REGARDLESS OF THE TIME!

Gil – (xxx)xxx-xxxx

Send was clicked upon and off it went. The bridge to where the real Tangerine existed had just been crossed, trusting that it hadn't been consumed by the possibility of a burning. Gil had mixed feelings of what he had just done. But, whatever. There was no going back now. He spoke and she will eventually hear. More accurately described, he typed and she will eventually read.

The list of possibilities scrolled through his head: It may be a while before she even receives his response; she may be so pissed by now by his further demonstration of rejection through his weeks of no responsiveness that when the e-mail comes, it may be met with a "fuck-off" attitude; or the phone could ring at any moment. She may have been waiting and longing for such an invitation and without delay take it. That possibility scared the hell out of him. All to well, Gil knew optimistic expectations were dangerous. For him, they are the planks one walks blindly on towards the inevitable drop off. To think she may call, and call soon, implacably attached him to an anticipation that positioned him in a subservient lot where he unwittingly submitted himself to an inanimate prepotency that he knew he couldn't psychologically or emotionally afford to tamper with. However, it was all too late. The die was cast. The laws of cause and effect had been set in motion the second he clicked on send and each second that passed thereafter, momentum was spinning his wheels beyond control.

December 19th. A little under a week before the celebrated birth of Christ, the Christmas Emmanuel and nearing the forty-eight hour mark since Gil's response to Tangerine's e-mail was sent off. Still, no reply from her end.

Diligently, he continued to check his e-mail.

Nothing.

Perking his sense of hearing, he listened out for the ringing of his phone.

Silence.

Gil preoccupied his time with business, warring off the all-consuming wonderings of her silence. All papers and exams had been graded; dishes washed, dried and put away; clothes washed, dried, and put away, and the front and back lawns cut, edged and swept. Still, no phone call, no voice mail message left and nothing in the e-mail inbox from one Tangerine85.

Every passing minute was one step forward towards the edge of the plank. The drop off was nearing, as was the fall. Manifested behaviors demonstrated his loyal enslavement to expectation. No blared music played in the house when at home, a usual accompaniment for Gil. Monitored volume on the TV when viewed was now enforced. All attempts to make the hearing of the phone a priority. The only tone that rang aloud was silence. One so loud that it pierced his heart to the very core.

The hollowed haunting of silence stayed with him. December 27th and still no phone call and no e-mail. With vigilant resilience, he fought to not be paralyzed by the unmet expectation. Although sick and ill from the whole self imposed affair, he managed to make due and take care of the daily grind that made up his standard life during the month of December. Some movies were viewed at the local theater. Dining alone at some of his favorite restaurants. Even a pop-in visit of a colleague had occurred. However, each moment spent away from the house, he couldn't seem to rid himself of the mental bombarding that accosted him of the possible message that may be awaiting him at home on his phone machine or e-mail inbox, which, to his let down, never came.

On the cold, brisk evening of the 27th Gil's need to eat caused him to set aside the novel he was successfully losing himself to, and seek gratification for his appetite. Not one to surrender his good-eating habits for justifiable junk in the name of holidays, he had thawed some chicken breasts earlier and pre-authored a chicken and veggie dinner, setting the table for the usual one. Before removing the chicken from the refrigerator, he was stopped by the artifact hanging on the refrigerator door that tangled beneath a magnet scribed with a quotable epigram that read, "A teacher effects eternity; no one knows where his influence may stop." An object of gratitude given years ago from an appreciative student. It was what the magnet held that prevented him from retrieving the chicken. Nothing artistically wowing. In fact, something rather simplistic, something containing nothing but remnants of a child's doings. It was a homemade Christmas card from Gil's son he'd received two weeks ago in the mail. To no surprise of Gil's. It was his fifth Christmas card from his little boy. Since the age of three, when Gil's son was able to author his own homemade cards through squiggled crayola artistry, Gil got, each year a folded-in-half crayon designed, construction-papered card that ended up suspended on the refrigerator door until January second when they were taken down and then stored away with the others in a drawer next to Gil's bed. This year's artistry was an attempted replica of his son's version of Frosty the Snowman standing amidst a handful of green crayoned Christmas trees with undersized and oversized red circles depicting Christmas bulbs within the green trees. Merry Christmas was written on the front, just above Frosty and the trees, every other letter in green and every other letter in red. Upon opening the card, in gigantic bold letters, the word DAD appeared with the A centered perfectly in the crease, splitting the A right down the middle and tangling the A's legs, one on each side of the page closely attached to the D's.

Gil stood, frozen, more frozen then the disproportionate Frosty he was faced-off with, whose two out of three bodily circles were more oval than circular, and whose orange carrot nose pierced the depths of Gil's icy-cold darkened soul. And from the two, black crayoned dots representing Frosty's eyes a message of longing for fatherly love from his son was being transmitted, penetrating into Gil's cracked, calloused heart. Fixated and vexed, Gil sensed that by willfully peering for further duration into this childish effigy, closer to the edge of the precipice he moved with only a step remaining before going over into the deep end. However, there was no turning away. Voluntarily he continued to peer while Frosty continued to judge and perforate. Brought to the brink, his stoned heart fell and cracked wide open, sending a rippling wave of remorse and morose throughout his being. Through welled up eyes and a melted resilience, he continued to intently stare at the snowman whose association held overwhelming significance and force that perpetuated the already-flooded-state with more gushing, rushing powers of repressed emotional onslaught.

Gil proceeded to bypass the snowman and gallantly unfold the card to openly reveal its inner contents; the word DAD. He placed the magnet above the letters, centered on the crease to keep the three red and green letters exposed without the intent of closing the card. Taking a few steps back, he cut his emotional vein deeper as he looked at his boy's inscription that unjustly labeled him as something he was nowhere near to being; a DAD. Anything but DAD. INFIDEL. SCOUNDREL. ENEFFECTUAL. SELF-ABSORBED BASTARD. COWARD. ALTOGETHER ASSHOLE. All of the above. But not DAD. Anything but DAD. DAD was highly undeserved. UNBEFITTING.

Deafened by the reverie of agonized reality, a faint sound brought him back to the kitchen and out of the condemning chambers of incriminating neglect. The sound was heard again, now in a more accentuated tone. A ringing. Again another ringing. Not a ringing in his ear. A ringing of his phone. Unaware of how many rings had already passed, he hurried and scurried like a sprinter out of the blocks to retrieve what he hoped wouldn't be too late of a pick up.

"Hello," he spoke with evidence of being winded and anxious.

"May I speak to Gil please?" The female voice spoke from the other end.

Gil knew who it was even before retrieving the call. By this portion of December, usually no phone calls came in. In the beginning and on Christmas Day is when the majority of incoming calls assailed the phone line. Invitations to parties, more than often declined or oral "Merry Christmas's" that were usually left spoken on the recorder and rarely reciprocated.

"Tangerine?" He phrased it like a question but knew it was she.

"Is this you, Gil?"

"Yes, Tangerine, it's me."

"Are you busy? Is this a bad time?"

"No, no, not at all," Gil stated, concealing his desperation to tell her not to even think of disconnecting. "Is everything okay?"

"Everything's fine. I'm calling as a response to your e-mail. I just opened it and called you immediately. I know you sent it a while ago, but I went up north for the holidays. Visiting family."

"How's the family?" Gil asked with little to no concern. A ploy to exhibit control that he had lost sometime back.

"They're fine. Thanks for asking."

"You're welcome," Gil spoke back, maintaining the small talk.

"About your e-mail, ...you said you wanted to talk about our last encounter," Tangerine phrased it in a way that was a gentle broaching of the topic. "And by the way, I was pleasantly surprised to receive your e-mail. Just sorry I didn't check my e-mail earlier. …I'm so glad you responded back…it's nice to be talking to you now."

Gil was taken back by her vulnerability. It seemed to display her as mature and courageous in comparison to his scared-shitless condition; her willingness to go beyond perimeters he only imagined crossing. In that instance he thought of what the French call *Bien dans sa Peau* – to feel at ease in one's own skin. This being linked to her. Not him.

"Yeah, …I was hoping to make some clarity of my sudden inappropriate behavior near the end of our time together and explain what was going on in my head. I know, maybe for you, discussing it is like trudging up the past, but I'd still like to meet with you and talk about what happened."

"You want to meet somewhere?" Tangerine said in a tone of surprise.

Gil was completely unaware that he had basically asked her to go out and talk about whatever needed to be talked about face to face rather than simply discuss matters on the phone.

"I guess that's what I mean. I mean…yes…that's what I mean. Are you free this evening?" Gil asked, unintentionally manifesting vulnerability through his cracks and not giving room for more delayed time.

"Are you free now?"

"Yes!" Gil quickly responded back, knowing full well that freedom of time has been the only source of freedom he has been experiencing, and that has been a burden on him; too much time on his hands, the gateway to obsessive imprisonment. Lately, emotional and psychological freedom has been the furthest feeling from his life. Attached to a woman half his age, plagued by desire for her, and the constant wrestling for emancipation from intrusive, havoc-reeking rumination of her doings and whereabouts were enough chain links to enslave him for a lifetime.

Too only make matters worse, guilt and regret for all his neglect had begun to make their way to the surface and weighted the already heavy load with a heavier burden to bear, making the sinking quicker and the despondency thicker. With nothing to lose and possibly salvation to gain, Gil said, "Yes, I am free at this very moment and would so like to see you, if that sounds fine with you?"

"It sounds perfect," Tangerine spoke with a tone of excitement in her voice. "Where should we meet?"

"I know this may sound a bit corny…but how about we return to the scene of the crime, the coffee house, and see if we can repair the damage in the location it was done."

"Nothing corny about that," Tangerine said. "I like the idea," which in fact she did. She thought it a romantic, redemptive quality. And a possible glimpse into a side of him that she had only hoped he possessed. "I can be there in about an hour. I need a little freshening up time."

"An hour it is. I'll see you then."

Gil hung up the phone and instantly felt an atoning resurgence course through his being. And in no way did Gil view Tangerine's unhesitant invitation for "now" and his unhesitant "yes" as pathologically impulsive; rather poetically spontaneous.

However, to his wit-of-mind, he heard Shakespeare's interlocutors Hamlet and Horatio contending on his behalf; remembering verbatim the lines he memorized in high school drama class

(more armor and ammunition for the young Gilbert to fend off the foes of facial malformation but never fully able to exorcise the fiends within)

when he played the lead role in the senior play Hamlet -

Hamlet. *Why, what should be the fear?*

…[she] *waves me forth again; I'll follow* [her].

Horatio. *What if* [she] *tempts you toward the flood, my lord,*

Or the dreadful summit of the cliff…

And there assume some other horrible form,

Which might deprive your sovereignty of

Reason,

And draw you into madness?

Hamlet. [she] *waves me still –*

…My fate cries out –

…I'll follow thee.

11

Night was seeping in, bringing with it a drop in the day's temperature. The holiday spirit continued to linger in the latter December air as stranger's faces adorned friendly countenances, ordering with neighborly delight their hot chocolates and a wide array of concocted caffeine elixirs. Bing Crosby and David Bowie's rendition of The Little Drummer Boy - just one of the many great hits of Christmas - played for those who camped their butts in various spots within the coffee house that would be theirs for the next hour or so, reading books, staring into a laptop screens, or conversing with others, all accompanied by a purchased product that represented their ticket to loiter.

Gil and Tangerine didn't get their exact previous location, but did get a semi-segregated table that provided the mild seclusion each had hoped for. Tangerine's attire was casual but classy, combined with her natural beauty, it was more than enough to take Gil's breath away the moment he saw her. Gil sported some Dockers, a black turtleneck, and a black petticoat, personifying the look of a stereotypical *intelecto*. Tangerine was also wowed by his appearance and instantly paid him his complimentary due. He, in return displayed homage to her looks by verbally acknowledged her glamour when they first greeted one another with a hug.

Both Gil and Tangerine were instantly infused with innocent-like excitement the moment they agreed to meet. Now, in the presence of one another, that same excitement became stronger and both did their best to contain it. Gil was much more successful than Tangerine. She, without hesitancy or reluctance, hugged Gil the first opportunity she got. Gil, taken by surprise, responded back with nothing but an action of reciprocation. However, during the brief embrace, he was surged by the power of human touch and didn't want to be let go in spite of his years of practice in the art of emotional detaching and concealment. Yes, he wore his iron mask like a gladiator, keeping in and kicking out any and all feelings that tried to merge or breech. Yet, Tangerine was a force to be reckoned with. The uniqueness of who she seemed to be and the possession of penetrating bedazzlement was an army Gil was in no condition to contend with. She weakened him, and paradoxically enough, he felt safe to be wrecked by her. Nevertheless, the pertaining words of Shakespeare's Hamlet once again rang aloud in his head as he felt the ghost of unrequited love:

> *Angels and ministers of grace defend* [me]! –
> *Be thou a spirit of health or goblin damn'd,*
> *Bring with thee airs of heaven or blasts*
> *from hell,*
> *Be thy intents wicked or charitable,*
> *Thou com'st in such a questionable shape*
> *That I will speak to thee:...*

"About what happened," Gil said after getting through conversational foreplay about their trivial doings over Christmas. Tangerine spoke of a warm family gathering up north, a longstanding tradition, while Gil fabricated a holiday that painted a picture a bit brighter than the dim, bleak truth he actually experienced. "Well, somewhere during our conversation, my wires got crossed. My emotions and mind became at odds with one another and I seemed to have lost control along the way. It's like I became someone else. Because of the internal mix up, I started acting strange, as you know. Not the person I was when we first started talking. And I was really enjoying myself up until my wires crossed. Does this make any sense to you?"

"Not at all," Tangerine bluntly said through a warm smile, keenly aware that Gil was trying to be vulnerable without being vulnerable.

"I didn't think so. It didn't make sense to me either. I guess what I'm trying to say…"

"What you're trying to say and what you're saying are obviously two different things. It feels more of what you're trying not to say. I believe your so-called crossing of wires is happening now. Willfully. You have something to say to me, but you won't allow yourself to say it in a way that flows from your heart. You're trying to stay in your head and it's not working. Come on, Gil," Tangerine said while placing her petite, gentle hands on his. "Talk to me from your heart. You can trust me. I won't bite."

Gil looked into her eyes as he was once again surged by her touch. In those tranquil, green eyes there was an honesty about her he could trust. A sanctuary for solace. Where else could he turn? There was no going back now. He had walked the plank, fallen off its edge, plunged into the vast unknown, had sunk and was going to sink deeper than he could afford, hoping so desperately that her tenderness, kindness held a kind of messianic reclamation.

"You are absolutely right, Tangerine," Gil stated while his thumbs naturally rubbed the skin of her fingers, exhibiting a concurrence through touch. "Before I tell you, from my heart, what really happened, you must understand, Tangerine…I stopped speaking the language of the heart years ago. Tragedy has that effect on the human creature. So for me to do what you're suggesting I do, even though it is, without a doubt, the right thing to do, it's frightfully hard for me. I am a rock of a man, Tangerine, an island, as Simon and Garfunkel sang it. To let things out or others in is a thing in my past."

"You're doing it now," Tangerine said, pointing out the transparency that Gil was unveiling.

"Again, you're right."

Tangerine gently and slowly removed her hands from Gil's and positioned herself in preparation for the receiving of Gil's spoken heart, providing him with an environment of safety and trust. In response, Gil opened his heart and permitted it to speak its language, a dialect he hadn't articulated in years.

"At some moment," Gil carried on, "during our conversation, I became very aware of how beautiful you really are. It was something I'd known the first day I called your name during role. Remember that awkward silence that everyone felt when I paused and basically stared at you? From that very instance, I knew the uniqueness that was you went well beyond the uniqueness of your name. But that day we met and spent quality time together outside of the school environment, I got the opportunity to truly look at you. To see you more clearly. Clearer than I've ever seen you. It was then that there came a moment when a heightened clarity of your beauty struck me, and I instantly became insecure by comparison. When those scales fell from my eyes and I beheld all that you are, it made me too aware of my own flaws and facial deformity, striking me with a sudden need to turn away from you, like a sinner face to face with holiness. In essence, I felt hideous, appalling and wanted to turn away so you wouldn't have to bear the uncomfortable burden of looking at me. Circumstantially, nothing had changed between us. It all changed from within. From within me. And I can understand why you would interpret my behavior at that point as switching to boredom or indifference. But I promise you, that wasn't the case. It was all me, Tangerine. I felt physically inferior to your perfected beauty and reacted as one scared of his own appearance. I guess I was trying to hide but had no hiding place to run to. I assume it was at that moment you opted not to tolerate what seemed to be my sudden state of indifference and made your great escape."

"And that was wrong of me," Tangerine quickly interjected, seizing the opportunity to right her wrong. "I should have addressed your behavior and explained to you how I was feeling."

"Should haves only come from hindsight," Gil said. "You did what you chose to do as a result of what seemed to be disrespectful behavior on my part. I do apologize for how I acted and the way I made you feel. Again, it had nothing to do with you. It was all me."

"Not necessarily all you. I'm the one who took off, remember?"

Gil gave Tangerine a gentle smile, acknowledging with agreement her role in their severed encounter.

"I have to say, Tangerine, since I'm speaking from the heart, that since that day we went our separate ways, I haven't stopped thinking about you, and God knows I've tried."

Tangerine responded with a big smile and said, "Really!"

"Really."

"I'm very flattered and happy to hear that I've been on your mind."

"Oh, more than you know."

"Why have you tried not to think of me?"

"Because I can't afford to want something I can't have."

"What is it you want and think you can't have?"

"You."

"And what makes you think you can't have me?"

Upon hearing this last question - ("*...what makes you think you can't have me?*") - his primitive loins were set ablaze by the possible gleaning of a seductive side to her.

"When viewed from a rational perspective, the answer is quite obvious. I'm practically, if not, twice your age. Hell, Tangerine, I could be your father. You are, or were and may again be, a student of mine, and I won't get into the ascetics of comparative beauty, that's an obvious variable."

"You're doing it again."

"What's that?"

"Staying in your head."

"This isn't rational thinking…me in my head, it's actual thinking, practical thinking. It's what I've tried to use to ward off my emotional reaction towards you…my developing attachment. And truth be told, it hasn't worked. I sought like mad to keep my desire for you at bay. To no avail. My Christmas holidays weren't good, Tangerine. Not good at all. They're normally not good but this year was much more difficult. I was constantly wrestling with thoughts of you, seeming only to perpetuate my desire for you and heightening my longing for you. Wanna hear something out of control? I read your paper… your essay paper. Not for academic reasons like a normal professor would, but for a sense of your presence, as though reading your written words would provide for me your voice of companionship, with the hopes that the longing for you would subside as a result. Pretty fucked up and out of control, huh? Well, I read it, and by the way, great paper, which I'd like to get into later. Needless to say, my presumed remedy failed me. It actually backfired. My attempt for comfort by your written companionship only served as a reminder of your absence. Then serendipitously a thought came to mind… the possibility of e-mail communication. Frantically, I went online to see if for some reason you might have made some kind of contact with me, not necessarily on a social level, at the least, as a student. Sure enough you did, addressing so honestly and maturely your feelings about that last encounter. You're e-mail bridged the gap between you and my need to speak to you. I instantly replied with anticipated hope you'd do the same. So you could imagine what I went through waiting for your response and not hearing from you until a few days later… not your fault, I know. Still, once I clicked and sent off my response, I was consumed by a relentless anxiousness that couldn't be shaken. Thankfully, you called. God knows where I would have ended up if you hadn't. Remember, this is just my attempt at honesty, not a plead for pity through desperate measures. I'm not saying I was at risk for any acts of stupidity, so please, don't get scared."

"No fear here, Gil," Tangerine said through what appeared a smile of appreciation. "You're just speaking from the heart, right?"

"Right."

"May I share a little of my heart with you?"

"By all means, please, before I drown you with my emotional bleeding."

"Of course, you know I had a reaction to your behavior and explained my reasons in the e-mail. But after leaving and thinking about how much I enjoyed our time together and your company up until that point made me regret my decision to take off. Even though I falsely accused you of acting out of sudden boredom, I wanted so badly to remedy the situation. That's why I found myself obsessing about it and wrote you that e-mail regardless of what you thought, even though I wanted so desperately for you to respond. To some extent, or to a great extent, like you, when I didn't hear back from you, I became disappointed and sad, wondering why you chose not to respond. Not hearing back from you made my Christmas a bit blue. And though I tried to shake off my thoughts of you and my underlying sadness by getting lost in my family and our holiday traditions, I still seemed haunted by my curiosities towards you. That's why I had no hesitancies to get in contact with you the moment I got your e-mail. Before I headed up north to see my family, I was like a junky, constantly checking my e-mail, hoping to find your response. While heading up north and spending a few days there, I figured you opted not to respond, and that brought another set of emotions and a kind of restraint from my constant checking of my e-mail. So you could imagine the joy I felt when I brought myself to check again and found your e-mail. Your e-mail and you being here now, in my presence, has made those past negative feelings null and void and has exceeded my desires and wishes that have ruminated in my head since our night ended on that bad note." Tangerine reached out her hands towards his as he reached back. "Thanks for being here with me, Gil. And thank you for speaking from your heart."

"Thank you, too, Tangerine…for doing the same."

And after diving so deep and spending some quality time below the emotional surface, they indirectly agreed and navigated their way back to the top and discussed matters not so close to the heart. However, briefly, they did submerge themselves back to certain levels of the heart's caverns when talking about Tangerine's paper and her experience with her father's marred face, which transitioned to Gil's history, dealings, and coping of his visual deformity. Tangerine exhibited her well-balanced ability to handle seeable imperfections. She did not try to evade or deny the obvious nor compensate with excessive compliments. In fact, at one point during his telling of bygone, bitter days of mockery and public ridicule, she caressed the mixed-matched side of his face and affirmed to him how handsome she thought him to be. Not just in this present moment. But from the moment he stared at her the first day of class. Nor did she make his handicap the central focus or find the need to have an over lengthy discussion on a matter that she rendered as secondary to who Gil was as a person and who he was in her eyes. And not once during their whole time together, even when talking about the artistic mistake God had made on his facial canvas, did Gil turn away from looking constantly in Tangerine's direction.

There was no place for inferiority in their ring of intimacy.

And for the first time in years, he felt safe. Maybe even saved.

In her eyes.

"Gil, I've noticed," Tangerine said as they furthered their conversation, "several times during the semester that you have worn a pair of Nimrod sandals."

"Very impressive. Most people have no clue how particular my sandals are. How'd you know they are Nimrods?"

"I have my own pair buried somewhere in my closet."

"Should I assume this means you've been to Israel?" Gil inquired with enthusiasm.

"When I was younger. My reason for not wearing my Nimrods anymore. They don't fit. So I just keep them for token sake."

"Wow! How old were you?"

"Around eleven."

"Why'd you go?"

"My parents. They were, not so much these days, world travelers and sought to raise me with a cultural flair, and so, as a child, I got to travel the world as my parents' way of educating me. Although academies, they believed experiential knowledge within the classroom of life impacted more than lectures in the universities. So…off to Europe, Africa, India, Egypt, and Israel we went."

"That's amazing," Gil stated. "Your parents are impressive people. I guess the fruit truly doesn't fall far from the tree. Did their means of acculturating you work?"

"Well, even though I was too young to fully appreciate the experiences, like I would now as an adult, I still greatly enjoyed the international ventures and would have to say I learned a lot, predominantly through osmosis."

"And how many times to Israel?"

"Oh, just once. That was their Middle-Eastern phase: Egypt, Israel, and Jordan."

"Does that mean you've seen Petra?"

"Yes. The Rose Red City carved by the Nabateans was one of the most amazing things I'd ever seen."

"Very impressive," Gil said, praising Tangerine for her knowledge on history.

"And you, you've been to Israel before?"

"Three times."

"Three times!" Tangerine surprisingly reacted.

"Educational reasons. I taught some courses as a guest professor at the Hebrew University in Jerusalem."

"Wow, that's impressive," Tangerine said, verbalizing a fact that she truly felt from within. Another reason for her to find him that much more attractive. "You just leveled up on the attractive scale Mr. Professor."

"Please, call me Gil," he bantered back, reciprocating wit.

"Gil. …Did you like Israel or was it a travel more out of obligation?"

"I love Israel!" Gil stated with passion orally pouring out of him. "The land, the rich history, even the peculiarity of the people, and not just the Jewish people, but also the Palestinians."

"Do you have a favorite spot in Israel? A location that moved you or resonates with significant meaning?"

"The land as a whole encompasses so much that it's hard to specify one favorite location. I spent a lot of time in the old city of Jerusalem, for the simply reason that the university's near there. The Western Wall, The Temple Mount, The Dome of the Rock, the different quarters within the walls, it's all inclusive as an ancient city experience, which I fell in love with the moment I entered the Damascus Gate. The Sea of Galilee, Nazareth, Bethlehem, and some of the holy sites within the old city, especially the Christian quarter with the Holy Sepulchral Church, although a bit too much for me. Too many people. Too crowded for my reclusive taste. But now as I talk about it, the Ein Gedi area stands out to me, with the Dead Sea, Qumran, and my highpoint, Masada."

"I assume you squeezed in your touring, or should I call them field studies, in between your lectures?"

"I only lectured about four times out of my two week stay, each time I went. Some of the residential professors took their spare time and escorted me through the land and told me places to visit. I actually spent a few days in Eilat, relaxing in Israel's beach resort. You've been to Eilat?"

"We never made it out there. I guess my parents didn't necessarily consider that part of much historical value, although we did make it to Qumran and the Dead Sea, where we mudded ourselves up and floated in the Dead Sea. Isn't that area with the tubs of mud and sulfur showers considered a spa resort?"

"Yeah."

"Talk about contradictory. Avoid Eilat but go to a spa resort. My parents. What ya going to do, huh?" Tangerine jokingly said.

"Can't live with them. Can't live without them." Gil joked back although he's lived without his parents for a number of years now. His father died a couple of years before his mother who died nearly ten years ago. Both from cancer.

"When was the last time you were there?"

"About eight years ago."

"So it's been some time. Haven't been interesting in going again or no invitations to teach?"

"I continually get invited to teach and I continually decline. My not going is more for personal reasons."

"Okay," Tangerine said, sensing that Gil wanted to keep the reasons personal and understood not to pursue the 'why' factor at this present time. She learned at a young age that "personal reasons" was not a welcome mat for further entrance. Most often an implicit no trespassing sign. "Any desires or plans to go back someday?"

"Someday. Maybe."

Just then Tangerine's cell phone rang with a distinct ring tone that identified for her a specific caller.

"Excuse me a second, Gil," Tangerine said, beginning to shuffle through her purse. "This could be important."

"Please, by all means."

"Hello," Tangerine said. "What was that?...Calm down, Lisa. ...Hold on, I can barely hear you. ...Let me step outside, hang on. Gil, I'll be right back. It's my friend, Lisa. She sounds very upset."

"No problem."

"Okay, Lisa, wait, I'm wal... ."

Gil sat there as Tangerine's voice faded out along with the distancing of her physical presence. Once again their shared time together was abruptly fractured. This time from forces outside themselves. So he hoped. Because, although there was no initial offense taken, Gil, however, pondered the suspicious possibility that the sudden phone call from her friend Lisa was a pre-meditated scheme to be used as a means for Tangerine to escape if the evening wasn't going all that great. The unexpected - or perceived unexpected - call would be the rescuing factor for Tangerine, turning a simple phone call into an emergency she'd have to attend to. Such a debased thought didn't last too long. Gil knew the evening was going better than expected and the glimpses of Tangerine's character alluded to the fact that she wouldn't act with such immaturity.

Tangerine returned after a short span of time and took her seat with a newly formed countenance. Concern weighed heavy on her face.

"Gil," she said with seriousness, "I'm sorry, but I have to go. Lisa is in some serious trouble and she needs me. I'm so sorry for this. I really am. I can only hope you understand."

"What is it?"

"She got injured at her job and seems pretty distraught by it."

"Can I be of some help?"

"Thanks anyway, Gil, but I don't think Lisa would approve of or appreciate me bringing anyone else. You sure you understand?"

"Yeah. Don't worry about me. You attend to your friend and call me later if you get a chance."

"I will. Thanks for understanding and thank you so much for tonight. I really had a great time."

Tangerine gathered her stuff and arose to leave. She kissed Gil on the cheek and quickly vanished from his sight. Not long after, Gil followed suit and headed home. No negative feelings were triggered because of the unexpected interruption. In fact, just the very opposite. Gil drove home and finished off the evening in a state of elated contentment.

A condition he hasn't been accustomed to in quite sometime.

12

When Tangerine found out how Lisa made her so-called living, she became concerned for Lisa's safety. She had Lisa promise that she would call her the instant something, if anything, went or was wrong. Lisa thought it sweet that Tangerine would exhibit such care but initially resisted the idea. Only because of Tangerine's refusal to take no for an answer did this become a consensual agreement. Tonight was the first time their agreed upon protocol had been implemented. The first time it had been needed.

There was no hiding the obvious. Tangerine instantly witnessed the bruised cheek, the dried blood around Lisa's left nostril, and the tear-stained face. These were only the visible markings. Lisa soon revealed the red, purplish welts that seemed to cover her entire backside, predominantly on the buttocks. She could barely move but able to cry vehemently. Tangerine cried with her while cradling her in her arms with a delicate touch so as not to evoke more pain.

Following the further breaking down in the security of Tangerine's embrace, Lisa told what had happened.

"He was a first timer," Lisa said, now able to speak. "He seemed nice and legit over the phone…even when he came into the hotel room. Good looking, well mannered gentleman, wearing a business suit…he presented well. Said he'd just got off of work. Also said he was more the sadistic type…got off more on inflicting pain than receiving it. My gut trusted him and wanted to render him quality service. He was fine at first, not much different than customers who've punished me in the past. But then, he drastically changed. Something came over him and his aggression became hostile…like he was no longer playing. From what I can remember, he mounted me and slapped my face with what seemed as hard as he could, like he was intending to slap another man. He continued to slap my face over and over…at some point, he must have cracked my nose because I felt liquid trickle from it and into my mouth where I was able to taste what I came to know was blood. I told him to stop, but he wouldn't. The more I tried, the more aggressive he became…as though my pleads were antagonizing him. He was a big man. Too big for me to handle. He overpowered me and my fuckin' purse was out of reach, so I couldn't mace the bastard!"

"Why didn't you scream for help?" Tangerine rationally inquired as her blood churned the more Lisa shared.

"I did! When he didn't stop slapping me after I yelled at him to stop, I knew I was in trouble…that's when I screamed for help…and as soon as I did, he covered my mouth with his monstrous hand before muffling me with tape."

"Oh my god!" Tangerine exclaimed. "What tape? Is taping your mouth part of your services?"

"It can be."

"Oh my god Lisa! And you supply the tape?"

"Depends."

"On what?" Tangerine asking with mild tones of agitation.

"On whether they are regulars I can trust and if it's requested and consented to prior to meeting so I can bring along tape. Tape isn't something I just bring."

"You said this piece-of-shit was a first-timer."

"I know."

"Then why the tape?"

"He had asked if he could tape my mouth at some point…before he turned on me…said it was a turn on for him. I was hesitant at first, knowing that by saying yes to his request I was breaking protocol. And I knew I didn't have any tape on me any way and figuring we were just role playing. So…I told him 'I'd like that'…"

"You told him what?...you'd like that!"

"Yes! I told him I'd like that. I was in character…you know, role playing…pretending…saying what he wanted to hear."

"Obviously he wasn't pretending."

"No shit!" Lisa responding, now taking on a mild defensive posture. "I told him I didn't have any tape…thinking that would end that topic of discussion but conveniently the fucker brought his own. Again, my gut tr…"

"You're telling me," Tangerine hijacking Lisa's flowing disclosure. "This asshole pulls out a role of tape that somehow you didn't notice he was carrying? Was it in his pocket? Or just tangling on his wrist like a bracelet?"

"He did have it in his pocket but not a role of tape…a single strip cut perfectly to fit over a mouth…my mouth. He pulled it out of his pants pocket and showed it to me…a single rectangular piece of duct tape attached to a piece of paper…I'm assuming so the tape didn't stick in his pocket."

"Oh my god!…oh my god!…oh my god!" Tangerine exclaimed now rising from her seated position and pacing about, displaying the bodies needed reaction to move it's highly charged, unsettled triggering's. "This is disturbing. Lisa, this guys a creep…I mean in the dark disturbed dangerous way. There's no way this is his first time doing this. It feels too pre-determined…methodical. Like there's a serial quality about him. How the hell did you not get the hell out of there the moment he showed you that?"

"As I was trying to say, my gut-instinct trusted him and consented… never suspected he would use the tape to shut me up. Even though I couldn't clearly speak, he knew I wanted him to stop. But the fucker didn't care. He got off more. After taping my mouth and slapping me a couple of more times, he then flipped me over and held my head down, face down into the pillows with his grizzly hand on the back of my neck, controlling my whole body with a single grip. …I thought he was going to kill me by suffocation."

"I'm surprised he didn't!"

"Listen Tangerine." Lisa stated, pausing her story to address the developing elephant-of-judgement that Tangerine was subtly ushering in to the room. "I know you support me in what I do for a living…and I love you for that. But I also know that deep down inside you don't approve of what I do for a living nor can you fully comprehend my encounters or experiences. And I know this must be hard for you to see me like this and hear what I'm sharing. And as an outsider looking in it's easy to think or say what I should have done or what you would have done…and this coming from someone who has never been on the inside of these experiences. You have to understand honey, my work causes me to encounter things, people you don't want to know exist…or only people you may read about in dark novels or psycho-horror movies. But I deal in reality…a different kind of reality…an alternate reality where secret selves come out to play…where dark passengers get expressed, even gratified…were primitive dobblergangers pay to temporarily get let loose and scratch their repressed fetish-itches and my job…my role you might say is to design and host a house of ill-repute for these creatures. And the truth is…I'm not much different than them." This con-joining statement from Lisa was not specifically in correlation to her vocational work as The Black Magic Woman. It was more in association with her own private fetish for the dead, which Tangerine knew nothing about.

Transparency does have its limits.

Tangerine took in Lisa's words and was cut to her core. She was able to read between the lines and realized that her initial care for her friend had turned in to advocacy for justice and resulted in judgement.

She had thrown a stone at her wounded friend from her own glass house.

With regretful-apologetic tears welling up in her eyes, Tangerine said, "I'm so sorry Lisa for coming across this way. I love and care for you so deeply and feel very hurt by what happened to you. And I'm angry…furious! Not at you…more at what happened to you…at the prick who did this to you. I wanna kill him! Rip his dick off and tape it to his mouth."

They both chuckled at Tangerine's avenging remark, softening the synergetic tension.

"Sorry…I'm not trying to justify my coming across the way I did… judging you."

"And I'm not trying to justify the mother-fucker in the name of occupational hazard."

"I know you're not. You're justifying yourself against my judgement, which you should never have to do because I should never be judging you. Again…I'm so sorry…please forgive." Tangerine said, her welled-up-eyes not dripping tears.

Lisa didn't have to say anything in response. The look in her teary-eyes and her motion to take Tangerine in her embrace conveyed atonement more than words could say.

Tangerine asked Lisa to continue explaining what happened, promising to do her best not to disrupt her with interjections, especially ones with judgement.

"…you were faced down in the pillow," Tangerine said, reminding Lisa where she had left off. "You thought he was going to kill you by suffocation."

"Yes…the nefarious-fuck was suffocating me…whether intentional or not, whether he knew it or not…and with his free hand, he slapped my bare body over and over and all over, my whole back and ass…while muffling my pleads for mercy and help in the pillow. It felt like he was flogging me, wanting to tear my skin off. Honestly, I couldn't tell if he was using his hand or an object…I guess I was desperately struggling for air I could no longer tell the difference…maybe I no longer cared. I thought he'd never stop and I'd never breathe again. Eventually, I stopped fighting him and rendered my self helpless. Maybe at some point, I rendered myself dead. I thought for sure he was going to kill me." After wiping away her tears and blowing her nose, Lisa carried on. "Finally, he stopped beating the shit out of me and released his hand from the back of my neck. I instinctively turned my head gasping for breath…it was all I could do. Through my nose, I sucked in as much air as I possible could, still barely able to inhale through all the snot and blood…it felt so damn good to breath. Trust me, I'll never take oxygen for granted again. And even though I was finally breathing again, I still had no fight left in me…I laid there waiting for the end of my life. I didn't know where he was. I could tell he'd got'n off the bed but I sensed he was still near and thought he was planning his final strike. I figured, in a few minutes, or maybe hoped that with in a few minutes he would finish me off and end it. I didn't move. I couldn't. I was so stunned by what was happening and the possibility of being killed, I froze. I waited and waited. He was killing me with the waiting. I heard him doing something, but what it was I had no clue. I wanted to turn my head and see what he was up to, but I was too scared. I guess I was playing dead. He must have been dressing himself the whole time I was waiting for him to get me, because the next thing I knew, I heard the door open and close. At first, I still thought he was in the room, but after waiting for what seemed like an eternity, I finally turned my head and discovered he was gone. I got up as fast as I could and locked the door. I peered out the window and saw him get into his car and drive away. I felt like I had no time to waste so I dressed myself, got all my shit and got the hell out of there. My adrenaline to survive and get the hell out of there must have numbed the pain because I didn't feel anything until I got near my house, then it hit me like a ton-of-bricks, I began to feel all the damage he had done. Then I checked myself in the bathroom mirror and saw that the prick literally fucked me up!"

"Did you call the police?" Tangerine asked with sincerity of care rather than inquisitive judgment.

"No. You're the only call I made."

"You need to go to the emergency, Lisa." Tangerine exclaimed, reverting back to statements instead of questions.

"I have no insurance, Tangerine. And I sure as hell am not going to wait in some emergency room with this severe discomfort until they call my name hours later."

"Did he break anything?"

"It's hard to tell now. By morning, maybe I'll know. My face feels okay. Just my backside, that's the worst."

"Don't you think you should call the police and file charges?"

"And tell them what, 'the guy that paid me to fuck him beat me up?' Come on, Tangerine, like they're going to give a rat's ass about a beaten up whore."

"You're not a whore, Lisa! And you have rights for justice. Who knows how many others the bastard has assaulted and how many more he will assault as long as he's out on the streets."

"He's what I call a Dark Lothario."

"A what?"

"A Dark Lothario."

"What's that?"

"A man who behaves selfishly…irresponsibly in his sexual relationships with women. I added the word dark"

"That's being nice! …you make him out to be some type of comic book villain…it sounds too complimentary…too much like a term of endearment compared to what that deviant bastard really is. He's much more than an insolent asshole. This guy's pure evil…all the more reason for you to call the police."

"Well, maybe someone else will bring him down. Right now, I could care less about the prick or any crusade for justice. I just need to rest and get some sleep. I'm exhausted and still very shaken up by all this. Would you stay with me tonight?"

"You have no choice. But first, let's attend to your wounds."

Lisa laid naked on her belly while Tangerine attended to her tattered backside with a wet cloth and some peroxide. Lisa initially flinched a lot but in a short amount of time was soothed to sleep by Tangerine's tender, loving care. Tangerine then left Lisa to sleep with hopes recovery would occur during the night. She then called Gil and left him a voicemail, informing him apologetically that everything was fine and that she would contact him sometime tomorrow.

The next morning brought increased pain and the need for professional medical-care. Tangerine dragged Lisa down to see a physician friend of her fathers; an arrangement Tangerine's father made for her after she told him of her friend's need for medical attention. One of the requests Tangerine passed along to her father when asking for help was no questions asked, by him and more importantly, by the doctor. And although exhibiting a face of shock and curiosity, the doctor posed no inquiry as to the cause of Lisa's bodily damage. He did his job and nothing more. He also waved any fees owed for the medical attention rendered.

Pro bono.

No internal damaged was found, but Lisa would need plenty of bedrest and specialized ointment applied to her backside three times a day. Tangerine would remain with her and implement the prescribed treatment plan until Lisa had more mobility and self-sufficiency.

13

Tangerine contacted Gil in the latter half of the day and explained, without details, what she's been preoccupied with for the last fifteen-plus hours. She also told him how much she had enjoyed his company and that he's been on her mind ever since. He dittoed her and said he'd like to see her again, soon.

"I'm sure you are, but, are you busy for New Year's Eve?" Tangerine asked, turning Gil's 'soon' in to sooner.

"Not busy at all. Why?"

"Well, my original plans were cancelled and I would like to spend it with you."

"Doing what?" Gil asked.

"Whatever. You have any plans or places you could drag me along to? Assuming of course, you'd like to spend the evening together."

"Tangerine, I would love to spend New Year's Eve with you. As for plans, well I don't have…wait, there is somewhere we could go. A professor friend of mine has an annual New Year's Eve party that we could attend. I haven't been in years…but from what I can remember, they're always great. Good fun. Would you be up for attending as my guest?"

"No. Only as your date."

"Sounds even better."

"Then it's a date?"

"It's a date. And…you're my date."

All the necessary arrangements were made for their so-called *date*. Gil would RSVP them (responding to the annual invitation he continually receives with a *yes - plus one*) and pick her up at her place. The time yet to be determined.

In the days that followed, between the twenty-eighth and the thirty-first, Tangerine and Gil spoke extensively over the phone, each enjoying getting to know one another a bit more prior to their scheduled *date*.

Meantime, Tangerine stayed with her dear, damaged friend and attended to her every need, loving her back to some level of wellness. It was because of Lisa's inability to move comfortably and the doctor's prescribed bedrest that granted Tangerine a vacancy on her calendar for New Year's Eve, a vacancy she turned in to an opportunity. Still providing continued sympathy and pragmatic care for Lisa, Tangerine housed within her a contained excitement for her anticipated evening with Gil. Gil himself was also infused with bridled enthusiasm and a resurgence of youthful revitalization, this in the face of the menacing fact that his salad days had been eaten away by impermanence and great loss.

By New Year's Eve, Lisa was much better and more able to fend for herself. Along with deep gratitude, Lisa permitted Tangerine to go back to her own place to stay and get back to her life. When asked of her plans for the night, Tangerine answered with uncertainty and vagueness, not wanting to yet divulge her with the juicy truth of her progressive involvement with Professor Patterson, the prick Lisa said she wouldn't mind fucking.

14

They both shone a new light unto one another. The light of celebratory fashion. Tangerine wore a fitted, red dress, displaying a more curvaceous figure than Gil had knowledge of. She appeared classy but not domesticated. Sexy but not scandalous. A good balance between Audrey Hepburn and Raquel Welch. Gil was adorned in a personally fitted, charcoal-gray, Armani suit, black, silk undershirt, and a predominantly black, with thin red stripes silk tie that coincidently matched well with Tangerine's dress. It was one of a handful of suits Gil owned that sat dormant for years in the back of his closet. A symbol of bygone days when he dressed for success that corresponded with a life full of riches that went well beyond a price. The two of them went together greatly and each was enamored by one another the moment of eye contact. In fact, Gil was rather stunned when Tangerine opened her apartment door.

"You look absolutely amazing!" Gil said seconds after she opened the door to his knock and on-time arrival. "Beyond belief!"

"Thank you so much. You look rather handsome yourself."

"Thank you. And these are for you," Gil said as he presented her with a bouquet of flowers he had concealed behind his back. "I hope this isn't considered old fashioned for you?"

"Not at all. I love them! They are so beautiful! Thank you so much Gil," she said just before placing a greeting-kiss on his cheek. "Just let me put these in some water and then we'll go. Come on in and have a seat. I'll be quick."

"No rush. Take your time," Gil stated as he took a seat. "I like what you've done to the place."

"It's not much," Tangerine said, projecting her voice from the kitchen. "But it's my place."

Upon taking a seat, Gil observed his surroundings. Not especially much to view. Little odds and ends, knickknacks, and pictures too far away to distinguish their contents. However, the place was orderly and well kept.

"Gil, these are so beautiful," she said as she walked out of the kitchen with the flowers now housed in a vase. After setting them on the small dining room table, she said, "How about the grand tour?"

"I would love one."

The tour lasted a total of about ten minutes, this including explanations of various items Gil inquired about pertaining to their significance. Not much to see in a small domain.

Henry's home on the other hand was big and elaborate, just like Henry's ego, Gil would jest on occasions. It had been eight years since Gil attending Henry and Lorraine's – Henry's wife – annual New Year's Eve bash. And never had he attended it with another. Only with his wife. His now deceased wife. And here he was, bringing a stranger in to a familiar space even though possibly feeling a bit out of place himself.

Henry was overjoyed after receiving the call that Gil would be attending and asking if he could bring a guest. Up until this year, Gil had declined each of Henry and Lorraine's invites although they never stopped inviting him. And even though Henry was sparked with ecstatic curiosity of who this *guest* was that Gil would be escorting, he did not inquire but had a strong inclination that it was the young woman Gil had spoken of; the single word *she* known as Tangerine.

"So this is what a professor's salary can buy," Tangerine said jokingly as they pulled up towards where the valet personnel was standing. "A lap of luxury."

"Don't be fooled," Gil responded back. "Lorraine is the real bread winner."

"Good evening, sir," the young valet said with a smile the instant Gil opened his door.

Gil responded back with the proper social protocol, "Good evening."

"The party is right through the front door, sir."

There was a time when Gil was a familiar face, addressed by his first name. Not tonight. He and the valet were unfamiliar with one another.

"Thank you," was Gil's only response.

"Enjoy your evening," stated the valet before pulling away in Gil's vehicle.

Following a deep breath and looking intently at the front door, Gil proceeded to enter, gently snatching up Tangerine by the arm in route and saying, "Are you ready for the lion's den?"

"About as ready as you are."

Little did she know and little did he show, he was nowhere near being ready, nor would he ever be ready. Cold turkey! That's all he was going on.

"What's wrong?" Tangerine asked when Gil suddenly stopped prior to ringing the bell or stepping through the door.

Gil's self-imposed ostracism from Henry's New Years gatherings over the past years made him question the freedom he once had. The freedom to walk right in without a ring or a knock. This current unexpected indifference froze him.

"Nothing," Gil stated, professing a white lie to his date, ultimately falling back on his friendship with Henry and opting to free access as once before without a ring or a knock.

And through the door they went.

The celebratory spirit was felt the instant their feet hit the interior floor. Clusters of colorful balloons adorned the ceiling, upbeat festive music played as background noise, laughter and twaddle chatter resounded throughout the house, silly, sparkly, glittered "Happy New Years" hats stood tall on the heads that wore them – predominantly the women – and drinks flowed out of bottles and glasses and into mouths that had no chance to encounter becoming parched. The environment was infectious.

For the good.

Gil immediately recognized familiar faces who in returned recognized him and greeted him warmly. There were also a number of new faces. People Gil did not know. Tangerine knew no one beyond Gil, and he, she has known shortly, but enough to take refuge in as she being a stranger in a foreign place.

"Well, well, well, Professor Patterson," Henry declared, sporting a party hat and drink in hand. "So good of you to come and grace us with your presence." Henry then went in and took Gil into his arms for a bear hug, which Gil reciprocated. Henry planted an endearing kiss on the side of Gil's face and stated after their splitting in two, "It's so good to see you, my friend."

"It's good to be seen," Gil spoke back.

Henry then turned to Tangerine and took her hand in the palm of his. "And this must be your plus one," he said and then kissed the top of her hand.

"Yes she is." Gil stated. "Henry, this is Tangerine. Tangerine, this is Henry."

"Nice to meet you, Professor." Tangerine expressed. "Your home is beyond lovely."

"Not as lovely as you sweetheart. And please, call me Henry. There are no professors here tonight. Gil," Henry said without turning away from Tangerine's eyes. "You failed to inform me of how beautiful your plus one is."

"Please, call me Tangerine." She witted back maintaining eye contact with Henry.

Gil smirked with a sense of pride that she displayed her ability and willingness to hold her own. Not in a defensive or condescending way. Rather, in a way to encounter and connect with Henry from where he was coming from.

"You're a bad man, Professor Patterson. A bad man. Come with me, my dear," Henry said, taking Tangerine's arm in an escorting manner. "Let me show you around and introduce you to some of the others. Professor Patterson, you could come too if you'd like."

"Please, call me Gil. There are no professors here tonight."

Gil smiled amiably as he watched Henry lead his date away from him and through the house, knowing all too well Henry's playful conduct, a personality trait of Henry's that Tangerine picked up on and willingly went along with. Gil followed the two close behind, condoning the comedic duet of his only friend, Henry, and his lovely plus one, the first woman he's opened up to since the death of his wife.

Tangerine conducted herself with elegance and grace, demonstrating a maturity beyond her age. Gil was highly impressed with the way she handled herself as Henry continued to lead and hold her up like a trophy. Gil later praised her for her natural behavior and found it all the more reason to open up and attach himself to her.

More than what already had been.

Eventually, Henry had released Tangerine from his clutches and touring and safely returned her back to Gil. Gil and Tangerine mingled with others for a short duration before branching off from the herd for some alone time. With a bottle of champagne and glasses, the two found a quaint, quiet spot Gil picked out; a balcony off the master bedroom that contained a spectacular view, where they became more *known* with one another over glasses of bubbly.

"You and Henry seem fairly close," Tangerine said, making an accurate observational statement.

"You can say that. About ten years now we've known one another. He's always been good to me, so has Lorraine."

"What does he teach?"

"Predominantly Cultural Anthropology."

"For some odd reason," Tangerine said in the process of pouring a second glass full for she and Gil. "His name together with the discipline he teaches makes him sound familiar. Have you ever talked about him during any of our conversations?"

"Not that I can recall."

"His face isn't recognizable. But I'm quite certain I've heard him mentioned by someone. Oh well, maybe it'll come to me later. Anyway... cheers, to a soon-to-be New Year."

Their champagne-filled-glasses made contact as they stared into one another's eyes with endearing intent, dizzied by the enchantment of the moment. Unspoken but conveyed was their mutual desire and willingness to fan the flame – the flame of *this* spawned liking for one another. Both non-verbally consenting to the possibility of new-love. Tangerine, being the younger of the two, had youth on her side. She lived with the euphoria of things-to-come, wherein dreams come true. Her posture-of-belief and optimistic-orientation afforded her the band-with to dwell in this luminal space, plunging headlong into the come-what-may of it all. Gil, on the other hand, resided on the back side of the wreckage-of life, whereon love and dreams had been dashed against the rocks of impermanence and subjugated to that universal *Truth*; everything that comes – even love and the illusory eternity of it – must also go.

The champagne continued to flow as their inhibitions continued to dissipate. Tangerine, who's always been an affectionate person, began to show truer colors and make physical contact with Gil during their conversations. A brushing of the arms, an occasional caress on the hands, multiple toying gestures, all seasoned with seductive stares. The one thing she did hold back and contain was the all-consuming-ever-present urge to kiss him. To kiss him had been a welled up desire for some time now. She even often entertained the fantasy of it; daydreaming of the delicious delight of their mouths fusing in to one. Although beguiled and tempted by the electricity in the air and the kinetic pull of their synergistic dance, she intentionally resisted the lure to kiss him *now* so as to save their first kiss for the midnight hour and enter in the New Year with *this* first believing it to be a good omen channeling many more *firsts* to come.

There was a boldness in Tangerine's inebriated state but not an uncontrolled surrender to the dark side of intoxicated stupidity. She was well aware of the things she was opening up to and able to possess the mental clarity not to ask about things that were not ready to be addressed. Now, for the longest time, Tangerine's curiosity about Gil's deceased wife and his son prodded her to inquire and discover the truth beyond the rumoring knowledge of hear-say information. Tonight wasn't the night nor was now the time. It felt to Tangerine that she and Gil were evolving to another stage in their relationship and she didn't want that to be halted or stifled by some beckoning curiosity.

Her tongue was bit.

For now.

"So, Mr. Patterson," Tangerine said. "The midnight hour is soon to strike. What are your plans for kissing time?"

"Kissing time?"

"Don't play coy with me mister. You know damn well what I'm speaking about." She stated through a zesty-silly little grin.

"Well, Ms. Tangerine, since you ask," Gil said as he turned to face her and took his own opportunity to exhibit his own uninhibited behavior by wrapping his hands around her waist and pulling her in close. "I guess I plan on kissing the closest lips to me, whoever that may be."

"Then you're not going anywhere."

Below them and floating out of the open first floor windows was the blaring sound of Dick Clark's voice from Time Square coming from the turned up TV, directing the in-house crowd through the countdown. In harmonic unison, voices blared the 10-down-to-1 New Year's Eve anthem, Tangerine and Gil joining the masses just above a whisper as they held one another, body to body, face to face, and stared eye to eye.

"10-9-8-7-6-5-4-3-2-1-HAPPY NEW YEAR!" Roared the crowded house accompanied with jubilant shots, quacking horns and then the collective sonorous singing that seemed to sailed through the universal airways

Should auld acquaintance be forgot,
And never brought to mind?
Should auld acquaintance be forgot,
And days o' long syne!
For auld la…

And just above a hush, the soft voice of the beautiful Tangerine spoke as a prelude to a kiss, "Happy New Year, Professor Patterson."

"Happy New Year, Tangerine."

They kissed.

Their *first* kiss.

The kiss of life.

Perchance a *New* Life.

Dear son…

Love,
your dad.

Printed in the United States
by Baker & Taylor Publisher Services